Somewhere
With You

BRITNEY KING

To: Rosie
Happy Reading!
xoxo,
Brittany

For my children and for everyone
who has loved the right person
at the wrong time.

Table of Contents

PART ONE

Jack

PROLOGUE

Most people would probably agree that ten year olds are impervious to falling in love. What does a kid know of love, they'd say. Most folks would say it's entirely impossible to meet your soul mate (and know it) at the tender age of ten, to fall head over heels, madly in love. But most ten year olds haven't been through what Jack Harrison has. If you were to ask Jack today, he would say that he knew more about love and loss and everything in between, even then, than the majority of adults roaming the planet.

It would be nice to tell you that Jack Harrison wasn't always the competitive, hard-nosed businessman most people know him as today. But to tell you any different would be a lie. Sure, maybe he was once a carefree, kind-spirited little boy, but Jack couldn't recall that version of himself—and anyone who might have, was dead. In theory, the shift had likely already begun the year ten year old Jack met what would become the love of his life.

It was the summer of 1990, a summer of record-breaking heat, the summer that he learned a lesson or two about what it takes to rise to the top, and exactly one summer after his mother had finally lost her five-year battle with cancer.

ONE

June 1990

Jack clearly remembers the first time he saw her face. He could easily recall that he was lying face down on the ground as a mixture of blood and dirt coated the inside of his mouth, one eye swollen shut, the other carefully fluttering, and then opening ever so slightly until he found himself peering into the bluest eyes he'd ever seen, eyes so pure and so blue that it was hard to tell where they ended, and the bright blue morning sky began.

They say if you are hit in the head hard enough, you'll see a beautiful burst of colors, and that is exactly what Jack thought he saw as he struggled to force open the one eyelid he still somewhat had control over. Later, he would remember that it was her voice he had heard first, the voice of an angel calling out urgently as he forced himself into a ball and lay there thinking of his mother. Surely, he told himself, that if she could survive all those years of suffering, then he could endure the next few minutes—it shouldn't be too long now until his bullies were satisfied with their work. He at least owed his mother that much, he thought.

Raymond Netzer and Joseph Coulter were well known among the campers for getting their way. You were either with them or against them, a sentiment they enjoyed reminding Jack of with each blow. They were a good four years older than he was, among the oldest kids at Camp Hope. That's the thing about death and the people it leaves behind. It changes them. You either come out better or worse afterward, one or the other, but never the same. Truth be told, there would always be kids like Raymond and Joseph. The world is full of them, bullies, up to no good. Death only added fuel to their fire. Jack and the others were merely an outlet for their anger, something to try to control where death had left them nothing.

For this reason, Jack practically begged his father not to send him away again this summer, because he was unfortunate enough to know what was awaiting him. But his father was unrelenting, insistent that Camp Hope, a bereavement camp for children who'd lost a parent, was where he needed to be. His father needed to work, he reminded him often, and not only would Jack enjoy all of the activities they offered, but he'd be out of the way, and best yet, it wouldn't cost his father anything. Maybe *you* should go to camp then, Jack had said.

"Can you walk?" the little voice asked.

Jack nodded his head.

"Here let me help…"

The girl pulled on his arm to no avail. "Come on. Get up before they come back."

Jack pushed himself up to a seated position and studied the girls face. She was younger than he was by at least a few years. He glanced behind her at the audience that had gathered. She seemed to have read his mind because she turned around then and thrust her hands palms up toward the sky as though she were demanding to know what it was they were looking at. She waved something he couldn't make out above her head. "You see *this* here?" she shouted. "It's evidence. Proof that you all just stood here and did nothing while those jerks beat him to a pulp! Now get to gettin'. Or else I'm turning these over. And you're all in for it!"

Jack watched the crowd scatter as he brushed the dirt off his pants, staggering a bit, as he made his way up to a standing position. He eyed the girl suspiciously.

She thrust her hand toward him so suddenly it startled him. "I'm Amelie. It's a pleasure to make your acquaintance. If only it were under better circumstances."

Jack furrowed his brow and shoved his hands in his pockets. He may not be as tough as the boys who'd just kicked the shit out of him, but he was no dummy. Jack knew exactly what he needed to do at this moment, for he'd learned very early in life the necessity of saving face. "No, trust me, kid, the pleasure's all mine. Now those assholes are really going to have it out for me." He looked her up and down. "Now, that a *girl* came to my rescue. I really didn't need your help. I would've been just fine on my own"

The girl seemed unfazed. "Well, I guess that's one way to thank the person who just saved your life. Oh, by the way, you're welcome."

Jack shook his head and turned back toward the hill. She followed. "Hey! You never told me your name."

Determined not to be seen with the girl as they made their way back to the center of camp, he picked up his pace as best he could given his injuries. "My name? It's 'as good as dead' now."

"Oh, come on, lighten up. Look on the bright side, will ya. You have at least one friend here now. That has to count for somethin', doesn't it?"

He turned on his heel and pointed his finger down at her face, vaguely aware of the onlookers. "Let's get something straight here, all right?" He motioned at her and then back at himself. "You and I… we are *not* friends."

Her face fell, but even Jack was impressed by how quickly she recovered. "Well... I just thought... I don't know anyone here... and... well by the looks of things, it doesn't seem like you have many friends... at least not anyone willing to stick their neck out for you, anyway. So, it appears to me that you could certainly use a friend or two."

Jack allowed the corners of his mouth to turn upward ever so slightly, which he was pretty sure didn't go unnoticed by the girl. She was young but smarter than she looked, he thought. And this would be just the first time of many that she would surprise Jack Harrison with her wit.

The following morning Jack received a pink slip requesting that he report to the camp counselors office. He entered the rickety shack and frowned when he saw the culprits who'd caused his black eye sitting beside one another looking none too pleased. *Wonderful. This is exactly what he needed.*

Mr. Thomas stood from behind his desk and motioned Jack in closing the door behind him. He motioned to the empty chair. Jack stood ignoring his wordless request. He knew what was coming, and he wasn't going to make it any easier than it needed to be. The best thing to do in this situation is to remain quiet and composed, saying nothing at all.

Jack stared at the floor. Mr. Thomas peered over the rim of his thick-rimmed glasses. "So… Jack… do you want to tell me what happened to your eye?"

Jack shrugged. "I tripped."

Mr. Thomas glanced at something on his desk. Jack's eyes instinctively followed.

"Uh huh. I see."

Jack squinted a little in an attempt to get a better look at the colorful object the counselor was eying. "Look, I'm on A.M. dish duty today… so if it's all the same to you, I'd better get to it."

The older man cocked his head to the side. "Jack, tell me… do you have any idea how poison oak could've made its way underneath the sheets of three of our campers beds. I mean… that's a pretty atypical place for poison oak to grow, wouldn't you say?

Jack considered the question for a quick second. "Well, we are in the woods here… so I guess you never know…" Jack was guilty. He knew it, and the counselor knew it. *How* he knew, Jack didn't know. But that wasn't the point. The point was to be as vague as possible, to give as little information as he could get by with— without either admitting or denying his guilt.

10

The counselor let out a quick, tired sigh. "Here's the thing, Mr. Harrison... I had to send one of our campers to the emergency room this morning due to a severe allergic reaction. The other two are sitting out there waiting for their parents to pick them up until... until they have recovered. Now, usually, I wouldn't have thought too much of this other than that it was an unfortunate incident. After all, as you've mentioned, we are in a heavily wooded area. But then this morning these showed up, coupled with a note." He scooted the items across his desk toward Jack. "Do you want explain these?"

Jack stared at the Polaroid's but didn't dare touch them. *Damn.* He met the old man's gaze head on. "What's there to explain? What's that saying? A picture is worth a thousand words? Yeah, that's it... a picture is worth a thousand words."

The counselor leaned back in his chair and folded arms. "Jack, I can't help you if you're not willing to let me. But you can't go around putting people in the hospital. Do you hear me? This is very serious. Bullying will not be tolerated here at Camp Hope. If these boys are bothering you, then I expect you to come to me. But you cannot continue taking matters into your own hands. Do you understand what I'm saying?"

"Completely."

"Mr. Harrison, one further question... do

you have any idea how these pictures might've gotten into my office? They came with a note… a very demanding note. But with no indication of who the sender might be. You see, it's my job to know exactly what goes on here within my camp, and if something is going on that I need to know about, I do not intend to be informed via a Polaroid photograph. Surely, you can understand my position, can't you? The trouble is that I just want to ensure that our little photographer understands it, too."

Jack smiled though it didn't touch his eyes. He shrugged his shoulders. "I have no idea."

The old man deadpanned. "Yes, that's just what I expected you'd say. Well, I guess now that we're clear here… you'd better get on to dish duty. Oh, and Jack?"

Jack raised his brow.

"It's dish duty for you for the rest of the week. Both A.M. and P.M. With one as creative as you seem to be, it's important that we keep all of that… talent contained. Now, one last time, are you sure you have no idea who sent these?"

Jack glared. "Your guess is as good as mine."

"Ok. Well, then… just to be safe, I'm thinking we'd better make that two weeks."

"Yes, sir." He nodded. "Am I free to go now?" The endless days of lying with his mother watching Perry Mason as she withered away counted for something, he thought.

The man motioned toward the door. "I suppose so. But do let me know if you can think of anything that we're missing here. About these photos, I mean."

Jack nodded.

That day, Jack scrubbed the dishes cleaner than perhaps anyone had ever cleaned them—thanks to that goddamned girl. He knew exactly who'd sent those pictures. And now, not only had she invaded his life, but his thoughts, too. He was going to kill her.

The next time that Jack saw the girl was in what they called 'group session' at Camp Hope. Jack hated 'group' where they were supposed to sit in a circle and 'talk about their feelings.' What the hell was there to discuss anyway, he wondered. Their parents were dead. They were in the middle of nowhere, misfits, cast off to some camp to 'talk' about feelings with strangers. Just so that the people who were supposed to really matter in their lives could avoid talking about them. It was what it was, so he never quite understood how talking about it was going to make any of it any different, which is usually why he sat outside the circle in the far corner of the room gazing out at the lake. Sure, they tried to make

13

him inclusive within the group, the first few times of which he politely declined. The third time he walked out on them all together and let the door slam behind him. After that, they'd mostly left him alone. This summer marked Jack's second year here at Camp Hope (which, by the way, he thought was a bullshit name), and it hadn't gotten any easier and certainly was not any more fun, the way they'd all promised it would be. He hated this place, though, truth be told—ever since his mother had died he hated it everywhere. Sure, Jack still loved his mother more than he loved anyone, but he was coming to find that even she was a liar. It wasn't getting better, and it certainly wasn't OK. She once told him that he could still talk to her, that she would be there for him. But it was all a goddamned lie. He knew by now that she wasn't really there. As hard as he might've tried, he couldn't see her, he couldn't feel her, and he couldn't touch her. She wasn't at a camp. She wasn't at a lake in the middle nowhere. And she sure as hell wasn't in any "group" circle time. She wasn't anywhere except in the ground where they'd put her.

Jack had been thinking of the letters when the girl's voice caught his attention. Although he was pretty sure she wasn't here last summer, he'd never paid much attention to whatever it was they discussed in their little *powwow* they held over there—but this time he found himself anxious to hear what she had to say. Whatever it was he was going to use it to destroy her. To crush her once and for all. Keep her out of his business, out of his life, out of his thoughts. Once is all it'd take, he knew this all too well. He watched as she stood and addressed the group. She was peppy, confident even—although not overly so. The good news was this was her weakness. It left room for people like him to create cracks, to manipulate the situation. But at the same time, she was the optimistic type. Nothing seemed to keep her kind down for long, and he hated her for that. These types of people were the worst.

Jack leaned back in his chair, crossed his arms, and observed as she casually flicked her blonde ponytail over her shoulder. She paused, looked up, and smiled directly at him. It was an evil smile with a lie behind it. *That much* Jack knew for sure. Whatever she was about to say, it was going to be stupid. He was going to hit the jackpot later when he rubbed it all in her face. As she spoke up, her voice cracked a bit but she recovered quickly. "I'm Amelie and I'm eight. This is a poem I wrote in honor of my dad. He was a famous poet. But now he's just dead."

The counselors smiled at one another, clearly a little uneasy and then nodded at the girl to go on. She was proud, her smile unwavering. It didn't even falter on the word dead. *This was go-*

ing to be so good.

"Roses are red.

Violets are blue.

My dad is dead.

If you're here... yours probably is, too."

The room was silent. The counselors looked nervous, wary. But the girl, she just smiled, and then glanced at Jack—or was it a wink? For a moment, he couldn't believe it. But then, as she sat back down, she curtsied in his direction, and that one movement solidified it all. The more he thought about it, the more he was sure that she had, in fact, winked at him. *Clearly,* this Amelie girl was messing with him.

TWO

Spring 2012

Jack Harrison stood in front of his office window overlooking the lake as he let his thoughts drift back to her. They somehow always did, whether he was here or not. Even still, this had always been the place Jack could feel her most.

No matter how many years passed, he could still picture her there underneath the tree that first summer, and though he could barely remember the boy he was then, in his mind he could still see her there under that tree, pointing her camera toward some unknown object near the lake. Whatever it was, she was forever looking through that lens. He never could quite see what the big deal was. He could remember how alone she looked sitting there that afternoon and also how like him being alone didn't appear to bother her all that much. He recalled how, finally, when he could not contain his anger any longer he strode over and stood over her, his hands on his hips, his expression fierce. Even years later, and though he would never have admitted it then, he could remember how sweet, how innocent, how beautiful she looked as she lowered her camera, looked up at him and smiled. No one had ever smiled at him the way she did—not before or after that day. It was a smile that implied: "I know more about you than you think I do." *It was a smile that meant it, too.* It was a smile that immediately saw right through him—that day and every day since.

"Why'd you do it?" he demanded.

She pursed her lips, brought her camera back to her eye, and resumed looking at whatever it was she had been looking at off in the distance. She didn't answer him for a long time, and the silence made him uncomfortable. Such a long time had passed between his question and her answer that Jack had given up hope that she was going to respond at all.

Finally, she spoke quietly. "Do you believe in things you can't see, Jack?"

He frowned. "No. But what does that have to do with my question?"

"Everything."

That summer was the first of many where he'd fight the urge to let the girl in and lose, after giving it his best shot. What he couldn't understand then was that, for the rest of his life, he'd be fighting to keep her in.

Over the course of those first few summers, they became fast friends—but with them it was always two steps forward, two steps back. She'd get too close, get on his nerves, and Jack would cut her off. That's the thing about Amelie. She always was an inquisitive little thing and damn it if she didn't incessantly hit the nail on the head when it came to people. She never pried. She didn't have to. She was the kind of person who made you want to tell her things. And what people didn't tell her, she somehow just *knew*. This quality fascinated Jack. He found himself drawn to it, to her.

The summer after Jack met Amelie, he still hated Camp Hope and put up resistance when his father made him go—but he never again hated it quite as much. For the next six years, his father insisted on sending him, and each year, he found himself putting up less and less of a fight. By the time June rolled around, he had looked forward to telling Amelie about all of the stuff he'd done during the school year, all the people he pissed off, and how much trouble he had avoided getting into. If he remembered correctly, it was somewhere around the summer he turned sixteen and Amelie fourteen that things began to change. Most of that summer he had been busy chasing a girl named Kristy (he was determined to get to second base) and Amelie was busy doing what Amelie always did, writing poetry and taking photos.

One particularly hot day, Jack found Amelie sitting on the edge of the dock alone, staring off into the water at nothing. He had also been particularly hot and angry that day as he'd tried and failed once again to make it to second base with Kristy. "What are you doing out here, kid?" he remembered saying. He had started calling her kid that summer because it made him feel somehow better than her. It made him feel superior—older and wiser, as if putting a name to it would make it so. In typical Amelie fashion, she didn't seem to mind in the least.

She didn't turn to look at him. "I'm thinking, JACK. You should try it sometime."

Jack plopped down next to her, playfully shoving her shoulder. "What's your problem?"

"I didn't have one. Until you showed up."

"Whoa. Have you finally gotten your period or something?" Jack held his wrist out motioning at the watch his mother had given him. "Because you know, kid, it's about that time."

She stood and glared right through him. "You know what? Fuck you, Jack."

"Geez, kid. Calm down! I was just joking.

What's your deal, anyway?"

She retreated a little. "I don't have a deal. Just stay away from me, ok."

"What are you always staring at out here, anyway?" Jack pushed himself up and grabbed at her camera. She managed to grasp it behind her back where he couldn't quite get to it, so he picked up her bag instead. She deadpanned. "Give me that, Jack."

Amelie continued trying to wrestle the bag from him as he playfully kept it away, holding it high in the air above her head. He was amused, and to her detriment, much faster, taller, and stronger than she was. "What's in here anyway? Your tampons?" She grabbed at it once more as he lowered it and raised it above her head again suddenly causing the contents to spill out. Jack's jaw dropped, and he stared at everything before him. There were dozens of photos of him. Of him and Kristy. There they were, plain as day—he and Kristy swimming. He and Kristy playing volleyball. He and Kristy eating lunch. He and Kristy around the campfire. Him laughing. Him frowning. As Jack stared at the photos, he noticed a strange look play across her face, though he wasn't sure what it meant. Was it pity? Remorse? *Hatred?*

"What the fuck is wrong with you, Amelie? This is sick," he shouted.

She stared at the ground, either unable or

unwilling to meet his eyes. "You're wasting your time with her, Jack. She's not into you."

Jack glanced down at the photos once more. He watched a few of them scatter in the wind and felt the rage as it rose in his chest. By this time, a small crowd of onlookers had gathered. He could see the surprise on her face as he grabbed once more for the camera. Maybe it was pure shock, but she didn't resist too hard as he took it from her hands. Jack turned the camera over in his palm, swallowed his anger, and then chucked it as hard as he could into the lake. Even now, he could still hear the audible gasp and picture Amelie falling to her knees.

"No, Amelie. Fuck YOU," Jack called over his shoulder as he made this way back up the dock.

"Jack."

He turned around slightly, but he didn't respond.

"That was the last thing my father gave me."

Fuck. Jack dove in head first, clothing and all, and swam harder than he ever had in his entire life.

Those words would be the last Amelie would say to him for the next three hundred and eighty-seven days. He knows because he counted. After the 'camera incident', Amelie refused to talk to him. Jack tried desperately to see her, but that summer, he learned another valuable lesson about women—when they've been publicly wronged, they tend to stick to together. There was no way any of them were going to let him get within two feet of her. Three days later, her mother picked her up a full month early from camp. Over the next year, Jack did two things: he wrote to her twice a week, and he worked his ass off to buy her a new camera. And it wasn't just any camera he planned to purchase—it had to be the best camera on the market. Up until that year, money had never been all that important to Jack. He despised any talk of money—mostly because his father seemed to be obsessed with the topic. But looking back, Jack saw the 'camera incident' as one of those life-changing situations you couldn't have possibly seen coming.

Jack's father was old school. If you wanted something, you had to earn it. End of story. His father was a successful stockbroker, hell-bent on teaching his son 'the business.' Up until that year, Jack couldn't give two shits about business. At the same time, he also abhorred having to ask his father for anything. In the case of the camera though, he found himself with little choice.

After a lot of persuading on Jack's part, his father finally agreed to front him the six hundred dollars he needed to buy Amelie the camera he wanted her to have. He'd taken the bus downtown several times in search of *the* perfect camera. He talked to sales guy after sales guy in order to discern which camera would be best. If he could just get *that* camera for her, he felt certain she'd be so blown away that she'd finally forgive him, and they could finally go back to the way things were. Before.

The caveat for his father loaning him the money was that he had to ride the bus to downtown Dallas every day after school and work for his father at the brokerage firm he owned. That was the year that Jack learned three things. One, his old man was an even bigger ass than he'd originally thought. Two, with money came opportunity, and without opportunity (such as with the new camera purchase debacle), you were nothing. And three, being successful in business provided one more power than you could possibly imagine.

That year, the year Jack turned sixteen, was the year he fell in love with the pursuit of money. Nothing mattered more, nothing less.

He was a quick learner, mostly because he had two things his older counterparts didn't: youthful charm (or perhaps it was ignorance, because he didn't know quite when to take no for an answer) and two, he had the drive they seemed to have lost somewhere along the way.

After three days, he'd earned enough to pay

his father back, and after three weeks enough to buy his first car. A car, which his father insisted he negotiate the deal all on his own. When he showed up in his brand new car, and told his father what he'd paid for it, his old man laughed in his face, insisted he read the terms of the agreement, and return the car if it were plausible. He was a fool, his father said, laughing in his face. It was that experience, the experience of heading back to the dealership and handing over the keys, that made Jack sure of one thing: it was the last time he'd allow himself to be screwed over in business. Ever.

With the second car, Jack did his research. He put in phone call after phone call, learning the base-price car dealers paid manufacturers to obtain the vehicle he wanted to purchase. He then negotiated solely by phone, refusing to set foot in the dealership until the said base price was agreed upon. When Jack showed up in his brand new Mustang GT and told his Pops the price he'd paid, and exactly the method he used to arrive at that figure, his old man patted him on the back. It was the first time in as long as Jack could remember that his father put his hands on him for anything good. He never did forget that feeling.

THREE

June 1996

Jack put the top down on his GT, turned up his Kurt Cobain c.d. on the stereo and let the wind blow through his now longer grungy, dirty blonde hair as he drove the nearly two hundred miles from Dallas to Camp Hope. He'd been caught up by work stuff. There were just too many deals to close, and it had set him back by a week. Although he'd called several times, he still had yet to speak to Amelie. Her mother always insisted she was out, but Jack was pretty sure she hadn't always been telling the truth.

He pulled into camp shortly before dusk, checked in, and then asked around for Amelie. There were so many new faces that year. Jack hardly recognized any of them. Seventeen was the maximum age for campers at Camp Hope, and he'd just about aged out of the program. His only option for returning after this summer would be to come back as a junior counselor, which was pretty much the last thing on earth he wanted to do. He was here now for one reason and one reason only. He needed to get this situation off his conscience. His plan was to give Amelie the camera, and then get back to business at home. Unsure where else to look, Jack headed for the dock. He pulled the camera from his backpack and double-checked the wrapping to make sure it was still presentable. He'd wrapped and re-wrapped it several times each time a little more satisfied, but he decided he just wasn't good at that stuff. It was times like these he wished his mother were around. She had been the best gift wrapper around. Jack remembered how he'd admire his Christmas presents simply for no reason other than that she had made them look so damned good. It was these kinds of things you forgot about a person after they died. Mundane things that no one thought to remember until you needed them. But Jack found these were also the sort of things that cut the deepest. It was funny that a task as simple as wrapping a gift could throw him off kilter for an entire week—but it could.

Jack made his way down the big hill and took in the sight of the fiery orange sun setting against the fading blue sky. Just below, he could make out a few figures sitting on the edge of the dock with their feet in the water. He slowly headed in their direction, but the two seemed oblivious to his forthcoming presence. Sure enough, it was Amelie and with her tracing his fingers along her palm was none other than the douche bag, Connor Levine. Connor was a year older than Jack and now served as a camp counselor… Jack was almost sure. He had always been well known around camp for 'picking up' the younger campers. Obviously, picking up had little to do with what it was Connor really did. Jack stopped in his tracks when Amelie threw her head back and laughed at something just out of earshot. He swallowed hard and cleared his throat. Amelie turned, and then cocked her head to the side as though she might not be seeing what she thought she was.

Her eyes lit up with recognition, and she smiled that smile. As always, it cut right through him. "Jack. Hey. What are you doing here?"

Jack shoved one hand in his pocket. The other held the wrapped camera. "I… I called, and you never called back. I wrote… and you never wrote back. "

"Guess you can't take a hint then, can you, bro?" Connor chimed in.

As Amelie stood, her eyes met Jack's briefly, before she lowered them toward the ground. But Jack never took his eyes off her. "I just came to give you this…"

Amelie glanced up and hesitantly accepted

the package. "Thank you," she said, though it was almost inaudible.

"Open it."

Connor stood. "Dude, get a clue. Can't you see? She doesn't want you, man." He nodded at the package. Jack dared him with the expression on his face to touch it. She doesn't want your shit, either. Tell him... Amelie."

Jack felt his face growing hotter. He took a step closer. The girl standing in front of him wasn't the same girl who'd walked away last summer. She had changed. She'd grown up. She was just somehow very... different.

Amelie frowned. She seemed to be studying him just as intently as he was studying her. "You grew your hair out," she finally said.

"Yeah." He touched the camera. His hand brushing against hers caused something within him to light up. "Are you going to open it?"

She looked down as though she'd forgotten she'd been holding something. Slowly and meticulously, she began unraveling the paper. Her eyes lit up when she removed the last piece. "Wow. Thank you, Jack. This is really, really nice. I mean... wow. You really know your stuff. But... you totally didn't have to do this..."

Jack smiled. He hung on every word she'd said. "Yes, I did."

Connor sighed loudly. "Are we done with this little reunion? Amelie and I here were discussing something important."

Amelie stepped forward and threw her arms around Jack's neck. "I mean it, Jack... thank you." Unable to help himself he inhaled her scent then pushed back abruptly. He grabbed her by the shoulders and glared into her eyes. "Amelie. Are you fucking high?"

She laughed. "Maybe. A little..."

Jack dropped his hands from her shoulders and lunged for Connor. Unfortunately, Connor was quick. He ducked. So Jack drop-kicked his ass straight into the lake. "Jack!" Amelie screamed. "What is wrong with you?"

Jack turned to face her, his eyes boring into hers. "Ha. I guess I could ask you the same question. I really didn't take you for stupid, Amelie."

Amelie raised her voice. "Well, I'm so very happy to have proved you wrong."

"I never got the chance to say I was sorry... but I wanted you to know. In person. Clearly that was *my* mistake. Anyway, I hope the camera is ok." Jack shook his head, turned, and walked away.

If he thought this was going to be an in-and-out trip, though, he'd been dead wrong.

For the next week, Jack observed 'Douchebag Connor' parading his friend, his only friend—by the way, around camp. Connor was making a fool of the both of them. Jack kept his head down and tried to stay out of trouble, which for the most part meant keeping his distance. Until a few days later when Amelie left several photos for him in his camp mailbox. One of them was of her and with it a note that read: *I'm sorry. Truce?*

Jack turned the piece of paper over and wrote six words: *Tomorrow, noon. Dark Room. Come alone.* He stuck the note back in her box and spent the rest of the day alone in his cabin working and doing whatever it took not to think of her.

The next day, he showed up to the rickety shack, which had been turned into a dark room, where he found Amelie, already working. He stepped inside and leaned back against the counter. He crossed his arms and watched her as she worked. The longer he stared, the less it seemed he could make out what it was about her that had changed so much. Over the past year, she had grown several inches and quite obviously, filled out in exactly the right places. This bothered Jack more than he wanted to admit. She'd changed in other ways, too. The shy, lonely girl he remembered had somehow blossomed into a social magnet. He hated this newer version of Amelie so much that it pained him to admit just how attractive she'd become. From the way she laughed to the way she moved to the way the tiny blonde hairs stuck to the back of her neck—it was *too* much. It made Jack want to touch her, and it made him picture her in ways he never considered—and for this, he hated himself.

She nodded in his direction. "What's up, buttercup?"

Jack shrugged. "Nothing."

She raised her brow. "You wanted to see me... *here*... for nothing?"

He crossed and uncrossed his legs. "I think you should stay away from Connor Levine."

Amelie laughed. "Really? Because I was worried that you hadn't made your feelings transparent enough already."

Jack studied her for a second before speaking. "You've changed."

"It happens, Jack. People change..."

"And why are you smoking pot, anyway? You're too smart for that shit, Amelie."

"Says who?"

Jack moved closer. "Look. I know what I did last summer on the dock was wrong. I came here to apologize... and to try to make it right. Whatever that means. I'm leaving in the morning but before I go, I need to know that you're going to stay away from Levine. He only wants one thing from you, kid. And we both know what that is. It's no different from the others."

"And your point is...?"

Jack sighed. "That you're too good for him."

Amelie pinned the photographs up to dry and turned to him. "I happen to like Connor. And I also happen to like getting high. Why do you care so much, anyway? Is Kristy too busy for you this summer?"

He rolled his eyes. "This has nothing to do with Kristy."

Amelie hurled a clothespin at him and picked up another. "Oh, but doesn't it?"

He ducked. "What are you talking about?"

"Seriously." She cocked her head and put her hands on her hips. "Seriously? You *really* don't get it, do you? I liked you, Jack. Hell, I may have even been in love with you. But you don't give two fucks about me. And what I realized later was that maybe you never did. Even before Kristy. It's as if I'm invisible, Jack. It's always about you. *What does Jack want? What does Jack think?* You never ask about me. Hell, you've never even asked how my father died. Everything has always been about YOU. And you know what? I've been ok with that. I let you be who you are because I care about you. I looked up to you. But you can't just stroll in here with your 'holier than thou' attitude and expect me to change who I am just because you're uncomfortable with it. You need to grow up, Jack. The world doesn't revolve around you."

Jack smiled and crossed his arms. "So you care about me, huh?"

Amelie shot him a go to hell look, threw up her arms, and turned her back to him.

He stood there for a moment watching her breathing return to normal. "I do know how your father died, Amelie. I just figured if you ever wanted to talk to me about it… that you'd bring it up. It wasn't my place…"

She put both palms on the table and leaned against the weight of her arms, letting out a long sigh. "Can I ask you a question, Jack?"

"Shoot."

She turned to face him, then perched herself up on the counter. "What is it like? The first time?"

Jack spat. He ran his fingers through hair then paced the length of the tiny room. "What the hell? We are not discussing this. And you are *not* having sex with Connor Fucking Levine. Do you understand me? Have you lost your goddamned mind, kid? SERIOUSLY! Have you?"

Amelie grinned, satisfied with herself. "Maybe, I have."

Jack paced back and forth. He went for a five-mile run and then swam laps in the lake. Just a few more hours, he told himself, until he could get the hell out of this place and never look back. All he knew was that if he didn't get out of here soon, he was going to kill that Levine kid. What was he thinking anyway, taking advantage of her like that?

Unfortunately for Jack, he knew exactly what he was thinking. And that was the problem. He considered his options: kick the kid's ass and be thrown out of camp, or leave on his own accord and let it go. Neither one seemed very appealing. In the end, he decided that if Amelie were going to be stupid, then she should at least be safe. Because god knows, Levine could really care less. Jack had heard him say as much. Pussy was pussy, and the girls almost never asked that he wear protection. Surely, Amelie wouldn't be that stupid. But she hadn't exactly proved him wrong lately on that front, so he needed to come up with a solution and quick.

As luck would have it, on his way to the mess hall for dinner, he spotted Connor Levine on the pay phone just outside the dorms. Jack placed his finger on the click button and flicked it. "What the fuck man?" Connor said, eyeing him before looking around nervously as the realization that the two of them were alone sunk in. Jack knew he had the advantage. People like Connor never faired well once they were singled out.

Jack slowly removed the phone from Connor's hand and placed it back on the receiver. "We need to talk," he demanded. Connor backed up just slightly. Jack slapped him on the back a little hard... enough to force the air from his lungs. Connor shoved him off, but Jack grabbed his shoulder and squeezed hard before letting go. He held up his hands, and Connor put up his fists. "Hey... hey. No, worries. We're just talking here. Man to man. Speaking of that, I need to ask you to leave Amelie alone."

Connor frowned. "And why would I do that?"

Jack chuckled. "Because I'm telling you to."

Connor stepped back further and put his hands up in defense. "Look, dude, I know she's your friend, and all... but if you wanted to tap that, then you should have taken your shot last summer when you had the chance. She was into you then, you know. And despite what you may think, I actually like this one. She's cool. Someone you can talk to, you know. She's got a good head on her shoulders. She knows what she's doing. Maybe you should give her a little more credit."

Jack gritted his teeth. "I'm going to ask you one more time, Levine. Let this one go. Or I'll beat your ass."

"Are you threatening me?"

Jack lunged for him. Connor stepped backward and held his hands up higher. "Whoa.

Whoa. I'm not looking for a fight, all right."

"How much?"

Connor smiled. "How much what?"

"Don't fuck with me, Levine. How much do you want? What's it gonna take for you to leave her alone?"

Connor paused and stared up at the sky, scratching his chin. "Well… as you can imagine, there are a lot of bets on this one. So far… and it's early in the game… I've got $550 on it."

Jack rolled his eyes. "Swear to me you won't so much as look at her again, and I'll give you $650."

Connor let out a deep breath. "$750."

"How about $650, I don't beat your ass, and we call it even."

"Fine. $650 it is."

"I'll have your money to you in the morning. Oh, and you can bet your ass I have eyes everywhere here. And if I so much as find out you come within fifty feet of her, I will personally see to it that you don't walk for a year. You got that?"

Connor rolled his eyes. "Yeah. I got it."

Jack thrust his hand forward causing Connor Levine to flinch. "Shake on it."

Reluctantly, he stuck out his hand and placed it in Jack's.

When Jack didn't see Amelie at their nightly campfire, he went looking for her. He wanted to say goodbye and ask her if she'd come up and see him later that summer.

He checked everywhere until finally, outside the dorms, a girl he didn't recognize called over her shoulder, "Rec Room."

Jack made his way to the rec room but found that it was dark and empty. Annoyed, he decided to make his trek count and retrieved two quarters from his pocket and placed them in the soda machine slot. Just as he slid the first one in, he heard laughter coming from the closet. Amelie's laughter to be exact. Jack stood there and listened for a second longer. As he got closer, he heard shushing, and then more laughter. Slowly, he opened the door as his stomach sank. Amelie practically fell over. She must've been leaning on the door. She, half-dressed and holding a beer can, while Conner Fucking Levine leaned over her and looked up wild-eyed.

"You mother-fucker," Jack called as he hurled his fist at Connor's face. He hit him over and over, as Amelie screamed and pulled at him begging him to stop. When he ran out of breath, he released Connor and watched him slump to the floor, bloody and nearly unconscious.

"What the fuck, Jack," Amelie demanded.

Jack grabbed her chin, and then let go as she

pulled back. He placed his hands on both sides of her face. "Amelie. Look at me. You're drunk and you're about to be in deep shit. Do you understand what I'm saying?" She nodded slightly. "Good. Now, here's what I want you to do. Listen to me carefully, ok?" Her eyes wide, she nodded again. "I want you to go to your room and pack your stuff. Discreetly. Don't let anyone see what it is you're doing. And don't say anything to anyone. Do you hear me? I want you to meet me behind the guy's dorms in ten minutes. All right?"

Amelie shook her head and glanced down at Connor. "But what about him?"

"I'm going to get help and meet you at the car, ok."

"I can't just leave, Jack," she said, her words slurred.

Jack placed his hand under her chin and forced her to look at him. "Amelie, you're half naked and drunk. And high. They are going to kick you out regardless. And they'll probably get the police involved. You do get that, right?"

He glared at her and waited for her to confirm she understood. She began to cry, dramatically. This was the last thing he needed.

"Ok, then. We'll head out tonight and let you sober up. In the morning, we'll call your mom so she won't worry and tell her you decided to leave early, and that I'm driving you home.

Now, do exactly as I told you and meet me in ten minutes. Or I'll have to leave without you.

Dazed, she shook her head and headed toward the door. When she got there, she turned back. "Jack?"

He exhaled. "Yeah?"

"You are going to do the right thing, and call for help like you said you would, aren't you?"

Jack ran his fingers through his hair and pursed his lips. "Of course, I am."

FOUR

Jack quickly grabbed his bag. He'd already been packed. Now he just needed to double back through the woods to his parked car. The key was not to be seen. He didn't want to have to answer any questions. He'd already decided that they'd take the back roads to avoid having to get on the highway and potentially get caught. He waited for Amelie for what seemed like forever. However, according to his watch, it had only been ten minutes. By minute twelve, he decided she wasn't coming, and that he was just going to have to leave without her. His heart was racing as he slowly turned the key in the ignition. He made it half a turn before changing his mind. *That damn girl.* He could go back for her but what if she'd been caught? What if she'd flagged down help, and in the process, turned them both in? Jack slumped back in his seat and rubbed at his temples, considering his options. If he went back now, he risked going to jail for assault. He hadn't had time to really discuss a proper alibi with Amelie, and besides, she'd been so wasted that she probably wouldn't have gotten it right anyway. Not only that, but what if she had sided with Connor? Where did that leave him? In jail, that's where it'd leave him. *That damn girl. She would almost surely be the cause of his demise.*

Still, in the end, he decided he couldn't just leave her. He hadn't said goodbye. If she were pissed at him, and she would be he knew, she sure as hell wouldn't have anything to do with him once she sobered up and Connor got to her. He wiped the blood from his hand on the back of his t-shirt. It was swelling rapidly, so he took a spare shirt from his backpack and wrapped it. He grabbed the hoodie that was lying across the backseat and slipped it on, pulling the hood around his face. Jack got out of his car and again doubled back through the woods until he was at the heart of Camp Hope. From there, he weaved in and out of the buildings until he reached the girls' dormitory located directly in the center, closest to the counselor's office. The light was on, and he could see a few counselors sitting around inside. He knelt down and almost crawled across the path to the girls' dorms. Once inside, he high-tailed it to Amelie's room and knocked. There was no answer. He slowly turned the knob, surprised to find it unlocked and ducked inside. Amelie's roommate looked up startled.

"She was packing, and then all of a sudden she just started throwing up. Next thing I know she's passed out. I keep shaking her, but all she does is moan. I don't know what to do. I was about to call a counselor… but she reeks."

Jack rubbed his good hand across his jawline and took a deep breath. *Damn it. Fuck! He should leave her here. No, he has to leave her.* "Ok… ok… just let me think…"

"They'll call her mom. They'll kick her out."

Jack slumped on the bed. "No shit."

The girl shook Amelie again. Amelie rolled on her side and then promptly threw up.

He sighed and pushed her hair away from her face. "Is there any way we can get her out of here without being seen?"

The girl twisted her mouth and then bit her lip. "Um…"

"A back door? Preferably something on the wooded side of camp?"

Her eyes lit up. "Yeah. There's a door off the living room. It opens out back."

Jack stood. "Great. Go check the halls real quick."

The girl looked at the door nervously. "Most of them are at movie night by the campfire. I'll check… but what's your plan?"

"My plan is to figure out my plan while you're checking."

Although she tried her best to hide it, the girl

looked worried. "Nice plan. I'm so glad you've thought this through."

Jack handed the roommate Amelie's belongings and then picked Amelie up and carried her just beyond the edge of where the woods began. He gagged the whole way there. She reeked of a mixture of alcohol and vomit. He placed her on the ground and instructed the girl to wait with her while he pulled the car out of the lot. Once outside the gate, he pulled off near the pines, killed his headlights, and waited for few minutes just to be sure that no one had followed. It was a dumb move, he later told himself. A chicken-shit sort of thing to do, he thought. It was almost as though he wanted to be caught. His father would've laughed and said people who hesitate never win. Jack would've countered saying he was cautious, just going the extra mile. But his would have disagreed. His old man would've said he was a pussy.

Finally, Jack started out along the main road, doing his best to gauge where he might find a path that would get him back or at least close to where Amelie and the girl were waiting. Jack's only saving grace that night was that he'd run the trails in these woods for years and knew them like the back of his hand. Once he found a spot he was comfortable enough to park, he pulled over and made his way through the woods on foot using a flashlight that was almost burned out. He cursed Amelie the entire way. He cursed her stupidity and the trouble she'd landed him in. He cursed himself for even giving a shit. *Maybe his father had been right all along. Maybe he was a pussy.*

Once Jack made it back to where the roommate (he never did ask her name) and Amelie were waiting, he crouched down and sat for a few minutes trying to collect both his thoughts and his breath. He was pleased to see that while she was still passed out, thankfully she hadn't thrown up again. He picked her up and then placed her back down, wiping the drool from his shoulder. No way was he going to make it all the way back to the car, carrying her *and* her belongings.

The roommate seemed to have read his mind. You can take her stuff and come back. "I'll wait. But I'm not walking through the woods with you. It's too dark. Sorry."

"I'll manage," Jack said, with more annoyance in his voice than he intended to convey. He slung her duffle bag over his shoulder.

"Where are you taking her?" the girl asked nervously.

"Home," Jack replied, matter of factly. "Listen, not a word of this to anyone, do you hear? I'll have her mother call tomorrow and explain that she decided to leave early. But whatever you do in the meantime... do not tell anybody that you saw her like this, ok? Can you strip her bed and put it in the laundry? If anyone asks, just tell them that she got sick and called her mom. Say that's all you know." He reached for his wallet and pulled out a hundred dollar bill. "Here. For your trouble."

The girl searched his face, nodded, and took the money. Jack watched as she retreated back to camp not once looking back. He learned another life lesson that night: for the right price, people could always be bought.

Jack placed Amelie in the car, reclined the seat and pulled off her tank top. He dug through her bag, found another, and slipped it over her head. His eyes lingered longer than he intended. He couldn't help himself. He buckled her in, threw her soiled top in the trunk, and pulled out onto the road. He drove on for an hour or so before pulling off into a twenty-four hour gas station to fill up. He still had half a tank, but he couldn't keep driving unless he had something to perk him up. He didn't bother trying to wake

Amelie. She was out cold. Better to let her sleep it off he told himself. Inside, he picked up water, Gatorade, crackers, a map, a Dr. Pepper and a Snickers Bar for himself. As he headed to the counter to pay, he noticed the sheriff car pull-up outside, and two uniforms step out. *Please, please, please don't let them notice the girl passed out in my front seat he pleaded to no one in particular.* Jack quickly made his way to the counter and set his stuff down.

"These and twenty dollars on pump two, please."

The clerk nodded toward the parking lot. "Nice car. Where you headed?"

Jack gave the guy a look that conveyed he wasn't in the mood for small talk. "Austin." He motioned toward the car. "My sister and I are going to visit our dad. You know how it is… since the divorce, we hardly see him anymore. Of course, being the pain in the ass that she is, she had to go and get carsick on me. All over my mom's car, too. Who, by the way, is going to be *so* pissed."

The man flicked a dread lock over his shoulder and glanced briefly at the uniforms that were filling up at the coffee machine. He handed Jack a roll of paper towels and slid his change across the counter. He lowered his voice and quickly shoved the map into a paper bag. "Dude, I gotcha." He grinned slightly before straitening

49

his face. "No one's mother lets them take a car like *that* out on the road at this time of night," he said, nodding in the direction of the uniforms in the back. Jack briefly glanced in the anti-theft mirror overhead. Thankfully, the officers appeared to be focused on something on the television at the rear of the store. The clerk continued speaking, quietly, under his breath. "Anyhow, let's just pretend that pump two is broken. There's another station about thirty miles south of here. Can you make it?"

Jack grabbed the bag from the guy and took the paper towels. Clearly, the clerk was a little more experienced in matters such as these. "Um... Yeah. Thanks, man."

The clerk motioned slightly toward the door. "Safe travels, my friend."

Jack only nodded. However, for some reason, he desperately longed to tell the tattooed, pierced man standing opposite him that he was right. His mother would never have let him take a car like that out on the road, at this hour or any other. But it didn't matter because his mother was dead. He wanted to say the words, if for no other reason than the fact that the guy seemed like the sort of person who would understand such a thing.

Amelie stretched her legs, yawned, and suddenly sprang to life just after dawn. "I feel like ass," she said.

"You smell like it, too," Jack said, handing her the Gatorade and a bottle of Tylenol. "Drink that. And take two of those."

Amelie gripped her head. "I don't take pills."

Jack rolled his eyes. "Why's that? You don't seem to have a problem taking anything else."

"Well, smart ass... for starters, because the guy who killed my dad was high on prescription drugs." She shook the bottle and tossed it in the back seat as though it burned her hand just to hold it. "But also because these drug companies are just trying to get you hooked on their stuff, that's why. Hey! Where are we, anyway?"

"A few hours outside of Austin."

She gasped. "Austin! Why are we going to Austin? Jack! I don't want to go home. Why are you taking me home?"

Jack glanced over at her and frowned as he noticed that she'd crossed her arms and was in full-blown pout mode. "Because, kid. You can't seem to behave yourself at camp, and they were about to kick you out."

Amelie shifted her whole body in her seat a faced him. "Please don't take me home, Jack. Please."

"Where, smarty pants, do you suppose that I take you, then?"

51

"With you."

Jack laughed hard. "That's hilarious. Um, no. You are *not* coming with me."

"Why not?" she hissed.

"Well," he said, holding up his hands making quotation marks in the air, "for starters, because you are a pain in my ass who had caused me nothing but trouble for the past seven days."

Amelie slapped her thigh. *"Really,* Jack? Seven days? Exaggerating much? Anyway… as I recall, you were the one who busted in the rec closet and beat the crap out of my boyfriend."

Jack glared at her and then focused back on the road. "He's not your boyfriend."

"Whatever. If you take me home… I'm going to tell everyone that you kidnapped me. Because you did kidnap me, Jack. You know you did. You took me against my will."

"You were wasted, Amelie. And you are not blackmailing me."

She grabbed the wheel and turned hard. "We'll see about that."

Jack pushed her off and steadied the car before slowing and pulling off on the shoulder. He pushed his door open and went around to the passenger side. "Get out."

Amelie didn't budge. She fixed her gaze and stared straight ahead. "What in the hell are you doing?" he screamed. "You could've just gotten us killed!"

She leaned over and rolled up the driver side window. Jack rushed back to the front of the car as soon as he caught on to what she was doing. She locked the doors and killed the engine. "What the fuck, Amelie? We're not playing games here."

She smiled and held up the keys, dangling them in front of him. Jack's face reddened, and he pounded on the window. "You're dead, kid. DEAD!" he yelled.

"Take me with you. Promise me you will… and I'll unlock the doors."

Jack held up his middle finger and pressed it against the glass. She flinched but only a little as he slapped the glass one last time for good measure. It was futile. Amelie sank back in her seat and let her head fall back. Jack couldn't let her win this battle… that much he knew. He'd wait her out he told himself. He'd just sit and wait her out. He headed further off the shoulder, into the brush and took a piss. Then he walked a few feet further and sank down into the grass. He watched her down that entire bottle of Gatorade. Eventually, she'd have to pee. Until then, he'd just wait. Unfortunately for Jack, it was turning out to be a very, very hot day.

FIVE

Jack wiped the sweat from his forehead as the hot early July sun beat down on his back. He was growing angrier by the minute, and Amelie was apparently growing hotter by the minute. She'd cracked the windows just slightly, though still not enough for him to fit his hand through. Instead, she'd stripped down nearly to her underwear, which only further pissed him off. He couldn't *not* look at the barely dressed girl sitting in the front seat of his car. He couldn't decide whom he was infuriated with the most—her or himself for being attracted to her in the first place.

He folded his arms across his knees and rested his head there, pondering his options. At some point, he must've dozed off, because the next thing he knew someone was tapping him on the shoulder. He looked up, startled, to find Amelie standing over him holding a bottle of water. She was barefoot, in cut off shorts, no top, and a pink lacy bra. He stared at her hair tied up on top of her head and felt a feeling he couldn't place. *It was fury, he assured himself.*

"Here," she said thrusting a bottle of water at his face "Jesus. I can't believe you're so stubborn you'd rather die out here than take me with you."

Jack hesitated, and then decided he was too thirsty to be obtuse, so he grabbed the bottle, gulped the water, and refused to look at her.

"Fine. I'm sorry." She sighed. "There. I said it. Now, will you take me with you?"

Jack stood and brushed the dirt from his shorts. "You need to call your mother before she has the police looking for you."

"My mother's in Europe. Trust me, no one is going to be looking for me, Jack. Did you have to force me to say it? Is that what you wanted to hear? That she sent me to camp and fled the country? That I'm all alone…"

Jack sighed, unfazed. "Fine then. I'll just take you back to camp."

"Fine!" She called over her shoulder as she climbed back in the car and slammed the door.

Jack got in and started the ignition. "You have no idea how close I am to murdering you." He picked up her tank top and hurled it at her. "And put your god dammed clothes on, would you?"

Amelie slid the shirt over her head and promptly started crying. "I don't understand why you hate me so much," she gasped between sobs.

"What did I ever do to you, anyway?" Jack sat there staring at the blubbering snotty mess slumped over in his front seat, his mouth agape. *What in the world is happening here he asked himself? How in the hell did he get himself into this? And more importantly how was he going to get himself out of it?* After a few minutes, her sobs seemed to subside, so Jack put the car in gear and got back on the road. From the corner of his eye, he watched as she crossed her arms and pressed her forehead to the passenger side window as he made a U-turn and headed back in the opposite direction, back toward Camp Hope.

After a while, she finally spoke. "Jack?"

He looked over. *Damn, she was beautiful. Which is exactly why he was in this mess, he thought.* "What is it now?"

"I have to pee."

Jack pulled off at the next exit and into a gas station. Amelie looked confused. "Are we out of gas?"

"No. Why?"

She looked at him as though he were the densest person on the planet. "Because we're at a gas station."

Jack shrugged. "Yeah. You said you had to pee."

"I can't pee here!" she shrieked. "Gas stations are filthy. I'll catch god knows what in there!"

Jack shook his head as though maybe he hadn't heard her. "You're seriously shitting me, right?"

Amelie frowned. "No. I am not *shitting* you. I can't go to the bathroom here."

He blew out every last drop of air he had stored in his lungs and put the car in reverse. "All right, fine. Tell me... where you can pee then, Princess?"

Amelie pointed at a restaurant across the street. "Over there." She let out an exaggerated laugh. "Geez, you know nothing at all about women, do you, Jack? In the future, for the love of god and all women, puhleeze take a girl some place decent if she has to use the ladies room. We're not like you guys. We can't just whip it out and go wherever. Restaurants are usually a safe bet. Their bathrooms are cleaner than your average place because they have a reputation to uphold. Gas stations, they could care less. People buy gas regardless. But people generally do not eat in filth."

Jack rolled his eyes. "Great. I learn some-thing new every day..."

She winked at him. "Glad I could be of ser-vice."

He watched her disappear into the restaurant. Although he wouldn't go through with it, Jack knew if he were smart, he would just leave now and let her find her own way home. That girl was nothing but trouble. And he was in for a world of it.

After twenty minutes passed, and Amelie hadn't come out, Jack furiously went in after her. He found her standing just outside the restrooms on the pay phone. When she saw him coming toward her, Jack noticed something on her face shift, though he couldn't quite read her expression. Amelie abruptly hung up the phone and practically ran toward him with a huge grin plastered across her face.

"Who were you talking to?" Jack asked.

"Two things. First, what do you think of this voice?" She changed her voice so much she gave off a bad British accent. She didn't pause long enough to allow him to answer the question. "And I called Camp Hope."

Jack stared. "And?"

She clapped her hands and grinned. "And they bought it."

He stepped closer and grabbed her wrist. "They bought WHAT, Amelie?" Jack demanded through gritted teeth.

"Ouch." She wiggled her wrist away, stepped up on her tippy toes, leaned forward, and kissed him on the forehead. *His mother used to do that.* "Oh, Jack. *Jack, Jack, Jack…* you have GOT to lighten up. Come on, I'll fill you in in the car," she said and turned on her heel without waiting to see if he'd follow. He watched her walk right out the door.

Of course, Jack followed. *What choice did he have when she said his name like that?*

Back in the car, Amelie placed her hand on top of his. Jack stared at it but didn't make a move to pull away. "Ok, so… I need to tell you something. But first, you're going to have to promise that you won't be mad. Promise me you'll keep an open mind."

He pulled his hand away suddenly. "I'm not promising you anything."

"Jack, please."

He shook his head. "Nope. Just tell me what you did. No more games, all right?" *Whatever it was, of course he was going to be mad.*

"Fine. I'll tell you. But you can only freak out for a second. Just get it over with and be done with it, ok?"

Although he tried his best not to show it, Jack had to admit that he was amused. He cocked his head to the side and raised his eyebrows, but he didn't respond.

Amelie scooted over in her seat until she was so close he could smell the jasmine in her hair. *Oddly enough, it smelled of jasmine, and not vomit as he would've thought.* "All right... I called Camp Hope and pretended to be my mom. I told them I picked Amelie up... and by that I meant me, last night... because she... or I... *whatever... you get what I mean, right...* was sick. I said that Amelie called from a pay phone crying, and I just took her not bothering to check her out because, for one, I was worried and two, because all of the lights in the counselors office were off. And guess what, Jack? After giving me... who they of course thought was my mom... a very stern lecture about safety, and the importance of following procedure... they bought it. They freaking bought it! I'm free! We're free!" Amelie was grinning from here to ear. She was apparently so pleased with herself that she practically hurled herself into his lap. Her enthusiasm was so contagious that, for a brief second, Jack forgot to be mad. She studied his face, leaned up, and kissed him. On the mouth this time. And then, for reasons even he couldn't explain, all of sudden Jack forgot he was supposed to be mad at all.

SIX

Jack drove to a campground that a gas station attendant had said was located on the outskirts of town. "What we need is... sleep. And showers," he remarked as he pulled in.

"Definitely showers." Amelie smiled. It wasn't a bad place to stay. But it wasn't great, either. Jack parked the car and shuffled through his backpack. "Wait here," he ordered before disappearing inside a building clearly marked "Business Office."

Amelie opened the door, walked around to the rear of the car, and surveyed her surroundings. She stretched, undid her hair, brushed her fingers through it, and retied her ponytail. She rubbed her eyes. The day was wicked hot, the heat seemingly endless, and there didn't seem to be a breeze in sight. Jack emerged from the office, frowned when he noticed she wasn't in the passenger seat, and tossed a set of keys in her direction. She caught them mid-air. "Get in." He motioned to the door. "We're in number nine."

Amelie climbed back in the car and pulled her shirt over her head. *It was just too damned hot.* She shut her eyes and hung her head out the window as they made their way down the endless gravel road letting the warm air rush across her face. "There it is." Jack said, interrupting her reverie. She opened her eyes to see that he was pointing at a small travel trailer. "Our place for the night."

Her eyes lit up. "Whoa. That's awesome. I've never stayed in a camper before..."

Jack shook his head. "I guess there's a first time for everything, kid."

Amelie fumbled with the keys and unlocked the door as Jack hauled their things from the car. Inside, she proceeded to open every nook and cranny within the tiny space. "This place is so cool. There's like... everything a person could possibly need in here." *You would've thought she was visiting the Taj Mahal and not some shithole campground, Jack thought.*

This would be the thing Jack would remember about Amelie for the rest of his life. No matter where she was, she always made it seem as though it were the grandest place on earth. When he was with her, she had a certain effect on him that made him question whether or not it might be true. *This must be as good as it gets, he'd shake his head and think.* For the rest of his life, he never met another person who made him believe that more than she did.

Jack sank backward onto the tiny sofa and tried to tune her out as she rambled on. "Amelie, I have to head back to Dallas in a few days, at minimum. So I need you to consider what your plans will be when the time comes, all right?"

Amelie turned and looked at him nonchalantly. "All right."

"In the meantime, I need to get some sleep. You should do the same. I plan to head out pretty early tomorrow."

She opened and closed another drawer. "It'll be like a *real* road trip!" she exclaimed a little too enthusiastically. "Where to…?"

"Where is it you want to go? You know… with all of your 'freedom,'" Jack said as sarcastically as he could manage.

Amelie considered the question for a moment. "I don't know," she said and smiled. *There it was—that smile again.* Her smile faded just a little, and then she shrugged. "I was thinking… somewhere with you."

When Jack woke in the dark, it took him a few seconds to remember where he was. He squinted as he checked his watch, but in the pitch black of the camper, it was too dark to read the time. He pushed himself up and felt his way to the tiny bathroom. He flicked the light switch. *Damn. Too much.* He flicked it back off.

He fumbled around the camper a bit, and with no sign of her anywhere, he made his way to the door in search of Amelie. Except for the stars, he found that it was nearly pitch black outside, too. He stepped out onto the steps and stretched, allowing his eyes to adjust.

"Hey, sleepyhead," he heard her voice say. Jack turned his head in search of it. "Over here. To your right. In the hammock." Jack walked in the direction of her voice until he touched the side of the hammock. "Can you believe these stars?" she whispered. She patted the space next to her and scooted over. Jack hesitated, so she reached for his hand. "Here. Get in."

He climbed in next to her, trying not to touch her body to his. He adjusted his position several times trying to get comfortable before finally ending up on his back, his hands resting behind his head.

"Doesn't it all just make you feel so small, Jack?" He didn't answer. She didn't give him time. "This, I mean." she continued, motioning upward at the sky. "It's hard to believe we're just these two tiny specs in the entire universe. It's kind of crazy when you think of it that way, isn't it? Sometimes it seems like our problems are colossal and then... *this*... and you realize that in the grand scheme of things... maybe they're nothing at all."

"Hey. You think I can get that on a pillow somewhere?"

She punched his arm. "Geez. Why do you always have to be so serious? What is it with you? Really... Would it kill you to indulge me just once?"

He laughed. "Maybe. But isn't that what we're doing *here*, anyway? Indulging you."

She crossed her arms over her chest. "Good one, Jack. You should try stand up comedy sometime." She let out a long sigh. "Anyway, while you were crashed out, I went for food. I left you a sandwich in the fridge. Did you see it?"

There were so many things Jack wanted to say in that moment, things that he couldn't quite spit out. If his father weren't right about him, then these were the things Jack might've said: He would've told her that he hadn't seen the sandwich because getting to wherever it was she was at, was all he could think about. He would've thanked her for this, for being here, for everything. He would've told her that she was the first person he could recall in a very long time that made him feel wanted.

He didn't say any of those things though. Instead, he pushed himself up, threw his legs over the side, and ran toward the safety of the camper.

"Food? Did you say we have food?" he called back.

Inside the camper, Jack literally stuffed himself on all of the junk Amelie purchased. Junk, by the way, that he never would've eaten had he not been so hungry. His father always said 'you are what you eat.' Since he'd already consumed a candy bar the night before, this would have to be his last indulgence, he warned himself. Satisfied with his resolution and determination, he popped the tabs on two coke cans and made his way back out to the hammock. He found Amelie sitting up this time, her legs swinging back and forth over the side of the hammock. Jack could almost recognize the little girl in her, the little girl he'd met that first summer. Although hardly a little girl now, he knew she was still in there somewhere. He handed her one of the cokes and plopped down beside her.

"You know, Jack…" She started and stopped, before starting again. "I've been thinking…"

"Oh, shit." Jack chuckled interrupting her. "You? Thinking? That's pretty much guaranteed trouble."

Amelie frowned and then bit her lip. She straightened and shifted to face him. "Are you going to let me finish or not?"

He chugged his coke. "Finish."

"So… I've given this a lot of thought. And… I think you and I should just have sex and get it over with."

Jack swallowed hard and choked as it went down the wrong way. "Um. No," he managed when he finally recovered.

She glared at him with a determined expression written across her face. "So... what you're saying, Jack Harrison... is that you don't want to fuck me?"

Jack looked away. *Never look away, he reminded himself.* "No. Amelie. I do not want to fuck you." *Other things he thought, but not fuck.*

She dumped what remained of her coke, carefully removed his drink from his hand, and placed it on the ground. She stood up, pushed him backward, and climbed on top, straddling him. Jack didn't resist. He was too amused and maybe even a little powerless to stop the train wreck which was surely about to happen. She pinned his arms above his head, and he let her. *Don't let it go this far, he warned himself.*

Amelie searched his eyes before a wide grin swept across her face. "Whew! Well. I'm glad. Actually, that's the best news I've heard all day, Jack! Because I was worried that we were about to find ourselves in real trouble here."

With one fell swoop, Jack flipped her over on her back and climbed off the hammock. "You're insane," he called over his shoulder, letting the trailer door slam behind him.

Several hours later, Jack froze when he felt the bed dip. Amelie pulled the covers back and crawled in beside him. He hadn't been sleeping, but his best defense he decided at that moment was to pretend that he was now. "Jack." She shook him. "Jack?" He mumbled and scooted further away. "Jack! Wake up! I can't sleep."

She wasn't going to give up, was she? Some small part of him was satisfied with the answer. He rolled over and faced her. "And? What is it you want me to do about it?"

"I want you to talk to me… please?" She sounded so meek that if he weren't so busy forcing himself to be annoyed, he might've almost felt sorry for her.

Jack shifted. "Fine."

She scooted toward him and curled her body around his. He stiffened.

"Tell me about her."

"About who?" *He knew exactly whom it was she meant.*

"Your mom." Amelie replied softly.

"What do you wanna know?" he asked with as much exasperation in his voice as he could muster. It had been so long since he'd spoken of his mother that he wasn't sure where to even start. He was also afraid that if he started speaking he might never stop.

"Whatever you want to tell me."

Jack took a deep breath. "She was beautiful and happy. And then one day she got sick. From there, she just got sicker and sicker... until any sign of the mother that I'd known was gone. It was as if she'd just faded away."

"I'm so sorry," Amelie whispered in the dark. "I've never really thought of it this way but... I guess I was pretty lucky."

"That's bullshit, Amelie. You weren't lucky."

"I really was, though. One day he was there. And the next he wasn't. At least, I can remember him the way he was, you know."

"Yeah, well... At least I got to say goodbye. I got a thousand goodbyes." *Jack was lying. Although he wasn't sure why. He'd never said goodbye. Even though he knew he should have said it, even though there were a thousand chances, he hadn't had it in him.*

"Sometimes... I feel like I can't picture him anymore. Like I'm forgetting him... I forget the way he looked when he smiled. The sound of his voice. The way his hand felt wrapped around mine. And it hurts so badly, Jack. It hurts *so* fucking bad. Sometimes, it's so painful I can't breathe. Like the pain just sucks all of the air out of me... until there's nothing left. I don't want to forget. I really don't. But I don't know what to do. I don't know how to make it stop. It hurts to remember. But it hurts even more to forget." She paused briefly. "Do you ever feel that way…?"

Jack pulled her closer and wrapped his arms around her. He let out the breath he hadn't realized he'd been holding. "Every single day."

SEVEN

Click. Click. Click. Jack opened his left eye, just barely peeking out. *He knew that sound well.* He pulled at the covers and yanked them over his head.

Amelie laughed. "Wake up! I got some really great shots of the sunrise. Oh... and I have an idea!"

"Do you *ever* sleep?" Jack grumbled.

"Hardly. If you must know, it's one of my best qualities."

He pulled the covers harder and tucked them under his head for good measure. "I'm sure."

Amelie toppled over him with a thud. "Well? Do you want to hear my idea or not?"

"So there's a choice?"

She slapped his back and pulled at the covers. "Of course, there's not. But you could at least play along. Anyway, so... I'm about to turn fifteen, and I've never seen a beach."

Jack peeled back the covers. "What? You've

never seen a beach? Ever? How is that possible? You live in Texas, for god sake..."

Amelie shook her head. "Never."

"So you want to go to the beach?"

She smiled. "Yeah, but that's not all."

Jack sighed and pulled the covers back over his head. After a few seconds, he changed his mind and decided to hear her out. He tossed the covers aside and sat up. "And why am I not surprised?"

Amelie searched his face as though she were trying to place something.

"What?" he demanded.

"Nothing. Anyway... here's my idea... You said you had two days before you had to be back home, right?" She didn't wait for a response. She didn't even pause to take a breath between words. "Ok, since we have two days, and there are two of us, I say each of us should get to pick where we want to go. And what we want to do with our time."

Jack looked confused. *That was her big idea? Seriously?* "All right," he said.

"Ok. Good. Now... here's the kicker. If my day is more fun than yours, then we make our little road trip three days instead of two." *And there it was. He should've known there was more.* She continued. "But if your day is more fun, you take me home. Just like we planned."

"And *how* is this in any way beneficial for

me?"

"Duh! For one, you get to have fun. Something I'm pretty sure you've never had."

She had been wrong. THAT was the kicker. Right to his balls. She thought he was boring. "You think I'm not fun?"

Amelie's smile faded, and her expression turned serious. "I wouldn't know because you're always so pissed off. Do you even know, Jack? What do you think? Do you think you are fun?"

"Yeah. I do." *Another lie.* He half-heartedly threw a pillow at her, and then climbed out of bed.

Amelie cornered him at the tiny sink. She sighed. "I'm sorry. I didn't mean to make you mad. I was just trying to be honest."

Jack looked down at her and smiled. *She wanted to bet... ok. Fine, he could handle that. It was too bad for her she didn't quite understand that betting was his forte.*

"Ok. But if I win, you have to promise me that you'll keep your virginity for at least another year." He paused and rubbed his hand along the length of his jawline. "Wait... you are a virgin, aren't you?"

The look she gave him told him exactly where he should go. "Why would I promise you that?"

Jack smiled. "Because you want to go to the beach. And I have a car."

She hesitated. He didn't. "And because apparently, you have no idea just how fun I *can* be."

Jack stuck out his hand. She smiled wryly and placed her hand in his. "Here's to you, Jack Harrison, proving me wrong."

He shook. "To you, Amelie Rose, for not proving me right."

Jack and Amelie took turns showering, turned in the keys to the camper, and headed south toward the coast. They'd decided day one would be hers (ladies first) since they were doing what she wanted to do anyway by going to the beach. They stopped to buy Amelie film and the snacks that she insisted upon—snacks that Jack was pretty sure would kill him before he turned of age. She forced him to at least try one of each of them, because it was her day after all. She also demanded that they stop to photograph every single thing that peaked her interest. She forced him to pull over so that she could photograph trees, bridges, cattle, and once a train.

Come on, she'd said. "Someday we'll have grandchildren, though not together, and they'll want to see these pictures. It's practically our duty to have as much fun as possible before we get old."

But Jack knew better. His grandkids would careless about seeing old photographs.

Since it was Amelie's day, she'd informed Jack that she also had control of the radio. She played and sang aloud to music that Jack thought might be ok, if one were mostly deaf. Although, the way she sang without reservation, the way she giggled when she got the words wrong, made Jack hate it just a little bit less. And though he pretended otherwise, Jack was fairly certain he was having the time of his life. *This must be as good as it gets, he told himself.* That, and he found himself noticing things he might not have otherwise. If only he hadn't made that damned bet.

He noticed the way the sun reflected off her hair, the way the blue sky matched her eyes, and the way her pinky toe was just ever so slightly different from its counterpart. To clear his mind, Jack put the top down and let his mind drift to nothing but the road in front of him. They drove on for a very long time without speaking. She reached for his hand, and he didn't pull away.

It was Amelie who broke the silence. "Jack?"

He glanced over and raised an eyebrow.

"Thanks for being my friend."

He eyed her legs propped up on his dashboard but quickly looked away.

"The pleasure's all mine, kid."

Amelie leaned her head against the passenger side window and soaked up the sun. She could practically taste the salt on her tongue and feel the sand between her toes. *She was so close, she thought. So close.*

Jack pulled the car into a parking lot that read Public Beach. He parked the car and turned to Amelie, who seemed worlds away. "So what's your plan?"

She turned suddenly and appeared confused. "My plan?"

Jack raised his voice but spoke slowly "Yeah. Your plan. Where are we staying? What are we doing while we're here? Where do you want to eat?"

Amelie slapped her forehead. "Oh! Yeah, how could I forget? My *plan!* My *plan,* Jack, is to have no plan."

Jack snickered. "That is quite possibly the dumbest thing I've ever heard."

"Somehow, I find that really hard to believe," she said as she opened the door and climbed out. She was halfway to the water with her shoes off before he managed to catch up. She plopped herself down in the sand, dug her feet in, and turned to him. "I don't get you, Jack Harrison. If you say you're going to let me call the shots, then let me."

Jack looked away toward the water. "I'm sorry. I thought I was."

She picked up a handful of sand and watched it slip through her fingers. "Really? Hence the twenty questions back there."

"Look, I'm just not all that great at giving up control. So sue me," Jack said, glaring at her.

Amelie looked out at the tide. "It's really beautiful, isn't it?"

"Yeah, it is," he whispered, not taking his eyes off her.

"Do you ever think of quitting, Jack?"

He studied her face, not quite sure what she meant. "Quitting what?

"Life."

Jack shifted his whole body toward her then. "Amelie. What in the fuck are you talking about?" he demanded.

"You know, doesn't it all feel like too much sometimes? Like it just takes so much effort... and you're not sure you have it in you to keep going. I think maybe I just *feel* too much. I feel so much all at once sometimes that it's overwhelming. So much joy. So much pain. And I just want to tap out, you know. To numb it. Or make it go away... I don't know. For once, I'd like to know what it would be like to feel nothing at all."

She seemed so despondent that Jack took her by the shoulders, pressing harder than he intended. He stared her straight in the eye. "No, Amelie, I don't. I've never felt that way. Never. You do know that this isn't normal, right?"

She gave a half-hearted smile. "What's normal, anyway?"

"Well, not giving up for starters."

"Then make me want to live, Jack. I'm telling you this because I need you to make me *want* to live. Because I'm honestly not sure I can do it on my own."

Jack exhaled and ran his fingers through his hair. "Ok. Just give me some time," he said. Even he could hear the desperation in his voice. Finally, he added, "You're right. We should do it your way. You'll call the shots. And the plan is that we have no plan. How does that sound…?"

She looked down at the sand and then back up at him. "Fun. It sounds like fun."

EIGHT

Amelie watched Jack as he studied the IHOP menu. It might as well have been the Sunday page of the Times, she commented more than once. "We're at the International House of Pancakes," she said grabbing for the menu. He leaned back, keeping it away. "What could possible be taking you so long to decide? It's really pretty simple, you see. We're here. You order breakfast."

Jack dropped the menu just a tad so that all she saw were his deep green eyes peeking over the top. *She decided a long time ago that he had kind eyes. Although, she would never tell him that. Jack wasn't the kind of person who wanted anyone to think of him as kind. That much about him she knew.* "It's the middle of the afternoon," he remarked. "Maybe, I don't want breakfast."

She scowled. "I just don't understand how anyone could *not* want breakfast. That's crazy."

Jack sighed. *And she thinks I'm the crazy*

one…

Amelie lowered her voice, leaned forward, and crept halfway across the booth. "I think we should check into a hotel," she whispered. "A really fancy one. You know… the kind with room service."

"Ok," Jack answered, his mind halfway focused on what she was saying, the other half clearly somewhere else. He organized his silverware in a neat line and picked up the menu. *He just needed to think. Why wouldn't she shut up and let him think?*

Amelie snatched the menu from his hands. "Well… aren't you going to ask how? I mean… we're not even old enough to get a room."

Jack knew that didn't matter. *People can always be bought.* He didn't tell her that though. He simply stared for a really long time until she broke the silence. Which was another valuable lesson Jack learned that summer—when you're dealing with women, it's best not say *everything* that's on your mind. The less you say, the better it is for you. He learned that women do not think like men. End of story.

She leaned in closer, further invading his space. "I have my mom's credit card. Don't worry, she never checks the bill." Amelie waved her hand around in the air as though she were swatting at something. Jack's eyes followed her hand. "Her accountant deals with all of that. So, any-

way, I've seen Home Alone enough times now...
I'm pretty sure I know how this stuff works."

He frowned, looking back at her. "I can pay
for the room, Amelie. We don't need your
mom's money."

"That isn't the point, silly. A credit card
makes us look official."

Jack massaged his temples. *Let it go, he told
himself.* He was tired and hungry and emotional-
ly spent. He ordered pancakes and decided it was
time to tell her his secret.

Jack parked in the lot adjacent to the hotel
where Amelie had insisted upon reserving a
room. He watched her as she got out and went in
all the while thinking what a terrible idea this
was. He leaned across the steering wheel and
rested his head on the steering wheel as he con-
templated what telling her the truth about him
would really mean. On one hand, she would likely leave him alone for good this time, but on the
other, she seemed so unpredictable, who knew
what she might do. He was lost in thought when
Amelie suddenly appeared out of nowhere, put
her face next to his ear, and shouted boo. Jack
jumped causing the horn to blow. He leaned back,
which she clearly took as an invitation to stick

her body half way through the driver side door. He looked at her, puzzled. *Had she lost her mind?* Amelie grinned from ear to ear and waved a key card in this face. "I did it! I did it! I did it!" she exclaimed, over and over, her eyes wild.

"You did it," Jack said, matter of factly. Honestly, he wasn't sure she *could* do it. So much so that he'd already planned what he would say to the front desk when he hit up the hotel across the street once she'd come back, and her (non!) plan hadn't worked out. Much to his surprise though, she somehow had managed to pull it off.

"Come," she said tugging on his arm. "I scoped out a back entrance you can take. I'll meet you at the room." She glanced at the key card and inspected it. "It's number… 420."

Jack put his palm on the top of her head and gently pushed it back through the window. He opened the door and stepped out. "I don't need to take the back entrance. They really don't care that much in these kinds of places."

She leaned against the car, looking deflated. "Maybe they do, Jack. How sure would you say you are about that, anyway? Ninety percent sure? Eighty-five percent?"

Maybe it was her smart mouth, maybe it was the fact she was talking to him in percentages, maybe it was the setting sun or the salty air blowing across her face, or maybe he would never know what made him do it, but Jack leaned forward, grabbed her face with both his hands and kissed her harder than he'd kissed anyone, ever.

When he finally pulled away, Amelie smiled, her expression clearly a little dazed. "So, I take it we're doing it my way." She smirked. Jack searched her eyes, his expression serious. He leaned in and kissed her again, slower this time. And although he still wasn't quite sure whether he wanted to kiss her or kill her, all Jack knew was that he couldn't help himself.

Jack surveyed the hotel room and turned back toward Amelie. "Um... Why is there only one bed?"

She grinned. *This was so like Jack, she thought.* "That's all they had available."

He turned and twisted the door handle as Amelie practically hurled herself at him, pushing the door closed. "Where are you going?"

"To get another room."

Her face fell. "Why?"

Jack shook his head, moved her hand away from the door, opened it, and stepped into the hall. "Because I need my space. That's why."

Amelie stepped in front of him. Trying with all her might to force him backward, she shoved her palms into his chest but he didn't budge. She spoke as her voice grew louder and louder with each word. "You said... you *promised* that we were going to do things my way."

"That was before," he said. He grabbed her wrist, swiped the key card, and yanked her back into the room to avoid a scene. Once inside, he let go.

"Before what?'" she probed.

Jack walked away from her, opened the curtains, and admired the beach view. "*Before* I figured out that I'm not sure we can be friends anymore." He glanced over his shoulder and then back toward the ocean. Amelie had her hands on her hips, and her head cocked to the side. He could tell even without looking at her face that she was pissed. Jack focused on the ocean as he stared out the window.

"OH? And why is that?" she finally asked.

He glanced back over his shoulder again, this time to gauge his effect. "Because I'm afraid I might be falling in love with you."

Amelie's face twisted. She appeared utterly confused. "And what's so wrong with that?"

It seemed the girl needed a challenge, and Jack had just decided he was the one to give it to her. He turned back to the window and smiled to himself. "Everything."

Amelie showered. Jack slept. Or at least pretended to, anyway. Sometime after dusk, Jack noticed her standing in front of the window toweling her hair. "Look at all the lights," she whispered to no one in particular. Then she turned suddenly. "Jack, get up," she ordered, her face changing when she saw he was already propped up on one elbow watching her. "There's a carnival." She pointed toward the beach. "Get dressed. We're going."

Jack climbed out of bed, showered, and dressed. This was a bad idea. *He hated carnivals.* As they rode the elevator down, Amelie didn't take her eyes off him. "Humor me, Jack," she said as she reached for his hand, and they stepped out into the night air.

At the carnival, Amelie insisted on purchasing corn dogs, cotton candy, and fried things Jack couldn't even name. She dragged him from one end to the other. She forced him on every ride imaginable, and she made sure to capture Jack in all his glory on film. On the tilt-a-whirl, they couldn't resist first base. In the fun house, he hit second. On the Ferris wheel, they worked toward perfection, learning how the other liked to be kissed—which Amelie practically turned into an Olympic sport—complete with scoring and all.

On The Zipper, she urged him toward third. And Jack humored her.

He couldn't quite put his finger on what it was—the lights, the smells or the sounds, but Amelie was in her element there. She came alive, more alive than he'd ever seen her. That was Amelie: colorful, exciting, and a bit crazy. From then on Jack would always think of her like a carnival, minus the bad parts. She would sweep into town and bring with her all the excitement one could handle. You'd have the time of your life while she was there. Inevitably, though she would go, and with her a little piece of yourself, part of your joy, there would always be next year, you'd convince yourself. And that was that. Jack hated carnivals. *They were too risky, he said.* This one, however, wasn't so bad. Unfortunately for Jack, there would be other carnivals in his future. But there would never be one that came even remotely close to comparing to the one that night. Little did he know then... he would spend the rest of his life chasing that feeling.

NINE

Amelie playfully pushed him backward on the bed. "Are we gonna do this or what?" she laughed.

"Amelie. This isn't..."Jack started to say. She fell on top of him held her fingers to his lips. "Shh..." she whispered kissing him, pulling up to raise his shirt over his head. *What the hell, Jack thought? Why not?* He kissed her back. He stood and picked her up as she wrapped her legs around his waist, and then he laid her back on the bed. He carefully peeled off her tank top, and then slowly pulled her shorts down, watching her eyes the entire time. Any change in expression and he would've stopped. He leaned in, kissed her belly once, and tossed her shorts to the floor. He kissed her again softly, asked her if she were sure. When she nodded, he pulled back and reached for his wallet. "Why are you stopping?" she demanded, breathless.

Jack held up the condom. "For this."

She grinned. "Oh. Right. Well, hurry up!"

Jack leaned down and kissed her forehead trying to buy time. *Why, he wasn't sure.* "Are you sure that you're sure about this, Amelie"?

She reached up, tugged on his chin, and pulled him down toward her. "Jack. I'm sure that I'm sure that I'm sure. Jesus. Now, stop talking so much. Unless, of course... you're into that sort of thing."

Jack smiled and took it slow, admiring every last inch of her. He wanted to get it right. He didn't say another word.

He did well, he thought afterward, as they lay there wrapped up in each other, a sweaty, tangled mess, neither of them speaking for quite some time. "Wow," she whispered when she'd finally caught her breath. "That was really... *something.*"

"Oh, yeah?" Jack asked grinning in the dark.

She inhaled and exhaled slowly. "I could spend my whole life here in this bed with you and be happy just doing that."

You could lead a horse to water, but you can't make it drink, his father liked to say. That night Jack realized his father was wrong. You absolutely could. He kissed her softly and then pulled back. "I've got good news for you then. There's plenty more where that came from."

The next morning, Jack kissed Amelie's face until she stirred. Her eyes fluttered open. "Hey," he said.

She looked confused. "What time is it?"

He checked his watch again. "A little before five."

Amelie, yawned, stretched and then rolled over, facing him. "Again?"

"No." He laughed. "I want you to come with me down to the beach."

She narrowed her eyes. "You want to go to the beach. Now?"

"Yeah. There's something I need to tell you," he said, his face draining of color.

She rolled her eyes. "Oh, Jack… always so serious." She got out of bed and made a beeline for the bathroom. "Let me pee and grab my camera, and we'll head down."

Once they reached the sand, Jack spread the blanket out and handed Amelie a bottle of orange juice he'd taken from his bag. She looked surprised. "How long have you been up?"

Jack watched her twist off the cap and chug the juice. "A while."

She sat it down and picked up her camera. Adjusting the lens, she pointed toward the water. "I love it out here. The color of the sky, the quiet melancholy feeling, yet there's still the sense of so much possibility. This has always been my favorite time of day. Just before the sun comes up."

"Mine, too." Jack remarked surprised at how she seemed to read his mind.

"Listen, there's something I need to ask of you. A favor…"

She lowered the camera and looked at him, obviously intrigued. "Ok?"

"But first, there's something I need to tell you. I need you to swear that you'll never tell another soul what it is I'm about to tell you. Not a single person. You have to promise me that, Amelie."

Amelie looked annoyed. "All right. I promise. Just spit it out, already. You're really starting to freak me out."

He took a deep breath and let it out. "I killed my mother."

She dropped her camera and glared at him. "Your mother had cancer, Jack."

"Yeah. But it wasn't the cancer that killed her. It was me. Essentially, anyway. I mean, I'm the reason she's not here. I helped her die. I hid her meds. I threw out the food she refused to eat. I lied for her. And I kept her secrets. Maybe if I hadn't done all of those things, she'd still be here today. It's just that… she told me she didn't want to live like that anymore. She begged me. She told me she was sorry, that she'd do anything she could to be there for me, if she could. But that she was sick, and she didn't want to be sick anymore. I didn't know what else to do, so I helped her. It's just, well... I know now that I should've done more. But I guess I just figured that if I weren't a good enough reason for her to want to stick around, then what reason would ever be? I just didn't expect her to die. I really didn't..."

Amelie wiped the tears from his face. "Oh, Jack. I'm *so* sorry. But you have to know... somewhere deep down that you didn't kill your mother. Cancer did. Cancer is a disease. A disease, which at it's very being, is designed to kill. You did what you could. But... a ten-year-old kid has nothin' on cancer. "

Jack shifted. He sat straight up and quickly regained his composure. "Anyway, she left me all these letters... and I just can't bring myself to read them. But I need to know, Amelie. I really need to know. It's killing me..."

Amelie looked at him as though she just had the best idea of her entire life. "I'll do it! *I'll* read them for you. I can help you... make sense of it all."

He smiled slightly and reached for her hand. *You can lead a horse to water, but you can't make them drink. What a crock of shit. His father was an idiot.* "Would you?" he asked.

"Of course," she replied toying with his fingers. She paused, looking off at the rising sun, before she turned back. "Oh, and Jack? While we're spilling secrets here... there's something I need to tell you, too." She sighed and continued. "I lied..."

He glanced at her sideways, urging her to continue.

Amelie bit her lip, and then smiled a little. "My mother isn't really in Europe."

Jack and Amelie spent one more glorious day together before he insisted it was time he drove her back home to Austin. Even to this day, he wasn't sure whether or not her mother knew about that little impromptu road trip. Knowing Amelie, he had a strong suspicion she probably didn't.

A few weeks later Jack mailed Amelie the letters. That fall he left for Princeton, where Amelie had promised to visit. There were many phone calls back and forth and several letters. But Amelie told him she didn't want to discuss his mother's letters over the phone. It didn't seem right, she'd said. It was too personal a subject, she mentioned once.

For Jack, everything got better when he went off to school. He loved college life. He was in his element there. He thrived upon the steep competition and regimented schedule it took to maintain at a school like Princeton. Mostly though, he was happy to be out from under his father's watchful eye and away from the house that contained so many memories.

One afternoon in late October, he returned to his room to find a message lying on his bed. He didn't get many messages, so he knew right away it was from *her*. He glanced down at the piece of paper aware of the fact that his heart raced at the mere sight of her name.

He picked up the note and read: *Call me. I'm thinking about going somewhere for Christmas. And I want it to be somewhere with you. I'm thinking San Francisco... Let me know if you can make it.*

For the next seven and half weeks, it's all he could think about—seeing her. The only way he could even attempt to focus on his final exams was if he'd just hung up the phone with her. They'd talk for hours, late into the night. Jack's phone bill was enormous, but he swore it was the best money he ever spent.

A few days before Christmas, Jack boarded a plane headed west where he met Amelie in the terminal at San Francisco International Airport. He waited anxiously as the passengers filed out toward the gate. His breath caught when he finally saw her. Somehow, she emerged from the jet way looking not only more grown up, but more beautiful than he'd remembered.

"I have big news. Big News!" she said throwing her arms around him. Jack kissed her cheek and took her carry-on from her hand.

"It's *so* good to see you!" she shrieked, squeezing him tight. "How was your flight? How are you?"

Jack smiled, really taking her in. *God, he'd missed that girl. No one else had ever been that happy to see him.* "Better now," he said when he could finally speak.

As soon as Amelie and Jack checked into the hotel, they promptly had sex. Which should have made Jack happy but it didn't. She seemed different in that regard. More confident. And definitely, less innocent. After they finished, he watched Amelie as she stood at the counter and reapplied her makeup. "I thought you weren't seeing anyone," Jack hissed.

She stopped mid application and eyed him in the mirror. "I'm not."

"So you're not fucking anyone else either then?" he demanded.

Amelie did a double take. "I never said that."

He threw his hands up. "So you are then. I

knew it."

She turned and faced him. "Did I miss something? Was there an agreement about that?'

Jack felt his face redden. "I didn't think we needed to."

Amelie turned back to the mirror and spoke slowly, matter of factly. "So you haven't slept with anyone, Jack? That's what you want me to believe? Because I don't. Not for a second..."

"This isn't about me."

She smiled wryly and met his gaze head on. "Isn't it?"

They were forty-five minutes late for their dinner reservation thanks to Jack's insistence on make-up sex—sex to which Amelie happily obliged. Well, truth be told, they did twice. Once to make up. And once more for good measure.

Of course, Jack had slept with others, he thought to himself in the cab on the way to the restaurant. He was a freshman in college, for goodness sake. He just hadn't expected her to. Still, out of all of the girls he had been with, not a one compared to her, not even remotely. His fraternity brothers liked to say that *pussy was pussy.* But Jack never saw it that way.

To Jack, sex with other girls was just ok,

never quite fulfilling. Kind of like an appetizer before the main course. All fluff, but little substance. Sex with Amelie, on the other hand, set him on fire. Not only was she the main course, she was dessert, too.

At dinner, they played catch up and made small talk. When their food came, Amelie cut into her steak and informed Jack all about some documentary she had watched on animal cruelty and how she'd since become a strict vegetarian. However, just this once, she said she was willing to make an exception seeing that this particular restaurant's specialty was their world-renowned filets.

As he listened to her go on and on about the specifics of exactly how and which methods were used to slaughter animals used for consumption—his own dinner suddenly became a whole lot less appealing. She, on the other hand, was devouring hers.

"So, how's Princeton treating you these days?" she finally asked.

"Can't complain... School's good. Work is good. You know... I was thinking. You really should come up when you graduate in the fall. There are lots of good schools out there for you to choose from."

Amelie glanced at the floor and then back at Jack. "Yeah. Well... about that. Remember how I said I had big news?"

"Yeah." He smiled. "It's just that I've been a little distracted ever since... anyway, what's up?"

She straightened her back in the chair. "I just received my acceptance letter to one of the top photography schools in the world, Jack! Can you believe it? I could not be more excited!" she squealed. "Like I could seriously die today and be happy just knowing I got in!"

"Wow. That's great! Is it the one you mentioned before... what was the name of it?" Jack asked as he moved the food around his plate with his fork.

She swallowed and shook her head. "No. This one's abroad. In France, actually.

Jack furrowed his brow. "Oh."

Amelie was so excited she practically levitated off the chair. "Yeah."

Jack cocked his head to the side. "So it's a four year program?"

She nodded.

"But you're going to wait for the school you wanted, right? Your first choice... God! For the life of me, I can't recall the name of it..."

She shifted. "Actually, I'm not. I've accepted... early. I leave just after the New Year."

Jack placed his napkin on the table and leaned back in his chair. Amelie watched his face grow red, his jaw tighten.

He leaned forward and lowered his voice. "So that's what this is? This little trip of yours?

It's a hey, Jack! Guess what? Fucking see you later, sayonara… trip."

Amelie was caught off guard by his anger. "Jack. No. It isn't like that at all. I… I thought you'd be happy for me."

He stood and slid his chair in. "Then you're *obviously* crazier than I fucking thought."

TEN

That Christmas, Jack and Amelie spent five amazing days together in The City by the Bay. When they weren't busy staying holed up in their hotel room, they'd hop on The Bart and putter around San Francisco, taking it all in. It was somewhere around Chinatown that Jack recalled his anger begun to fade. Over lunch in Union Square, he told her how much he'd missed her, how he'd thought of her every day. It was on a bench under The Golden Gate where Jack told her he loved her for the first time.

"Jack. Don't," she'd pleaded.

He shrugged. "But I do."

Amelie let it go, or so it seemed. She picked up her camera, removed the lens cap, and pointed it at the water. *Click. Click. Click.* "Yeah, but you know that a relationship between us could never work, don't you?"

Jack should have been angry then, he thought. Instead, he was amused, curious. "And why do you say that," he asked.

She turned to him then and placed her hand on his thigh. "We'd suffocate each other, Jack. This…" She pointed back and forth between the two of them. "It would consume us, if we let it. You have your dreams. And I have mine. Those dreams… Jack… I'm not sure they fit together so well, you know. One of us would want more, the other less and… it would just end up a mess."

"But we haven't even tried. So, I guess we don't really know then, do we?"

"*I* know, Jack." She hesitated. "And I don't want to ruin what we have. I don't want *this* to feel like work."

Jack smiled. "What percentage would you say you're certain of that? Ninety percent? Eighty-five percent?"

She laughed, shook her head, and slapped his thigh hard. "You know… Jack Harrison… I didn't think it was possible to like you any more than I already do. But when you're like this— meaning, not so serious, I prove myself wrong. Every time."

By then, light rain had started to fall. Jack took off his coat and wrapped it around her. "We'd better go," he'd said glancing up at the sky. Amelie snuggled up to him and pushed her head into his chest.

"What if we didn't… not yet." He settled into her. "Jack?" she whispered and snuggled closer as though it were possible. "I'm really going to miss you."

He sighed, tucked his chin to her forehead, and inhaled, trying his damnedest to memorize the way she felt.

The next morning, Jack awoke to find Amelie straddling him, her camera pointed at his face. "Merry Christmas, Jack!" *Click. Click. Click.* She snapped. When he groaned in annoyance, she let the camera fall down around her neck, and she lifted a package off the bed and thrust it at his face. "Here," she said. "I got you something."

He pushed himself up slowly causing her to shuffle backward a little. Undeterred, she raised the camera back up to her eye and resumed pointing it at his face. Jack gave her a look. "What? I want to capture your face when you see what it is..."

He carefully tore at the paper and placed it off to the side. He surveyed the contents. It was a book. No, it was *two* books. They were photo albums to be exact. He looked up at her, unsure what to say. *Thank you would be good, he thought.* But for some reason, the words weren't forming on his lips.

She took the one on top from him and

opened it up at its middle. "The first one," she cheered and then paused, "is of us. It's all the summers." Jack looked down and stared at the younger version of him on the page. In the photo, he was holding a fish and grinning from ear to ear. *Did he actually grin like that? Had he ever really been that happy?* She slowly turned the page, not taking her eyes off his, clearly trying to gauge his reaction. In the next photo, there he was painting a fence. Jack barely remembered painting that fence until now. But seeing himself there on the page, holding the brush, it all suddenly came flooding back. The way she'd talked his ear off that day. The way he handed her the brush in hopes that maybe it would shut her up. He remembered how furious he'd been when she got it all wrong. He thought of the way she'd thrown the brush and sulked off when he yelled at her for painting in the wrong direction. "Painting is a solitary sport," he had assured her. Jack smiled then as he recalled the expression on her face right before she'd taken her finger, dipped it in the red paint, and traced a straight line from his forehead all the way down his nose. He laughed at how she'd crossed her arms and grinned afterward, clearly satisfied with herself. "Take that, Jack Harrison," he remembered she had called over her shoulder as she stormed off. *Take that, Jack Harrison was right. One photograph, and just like that, everything came rush-*

ing back. She was that good.

"Do you like it?" She nudged his arm.

He didn't answer—not because he didn't want to but because he couldn't. His throat was too dry. "Here, open this one," she said taking the book from his hands and replacing it with the other. She adjusted it in his lap. He raised his eyebrows suggestively.

She read his mind. "That gift comes next. Pun intended."

Jack shook his head. He opened the album and froze. There they were—glued one by one to each page—all the letters his mother had written him. She studied his face and spoke softly. "I wanted to preserve them for you." She handed him an envelope. "But I also had copies made."

His eyes filled with tears as he stared at the words on the page though not really seeing them. Jack swallowed hard as the tears threatened to spill over.

Amelie reached for his hand and wrapped it in both of hers. "These letters are really lovely, Jack. Your mother seems like an amazing person," she said quietly, wiping the tears from her cheek with the back of her hand. "And I can tell that she really, really loves you."

Jack looked up at her then. "Loved. You meant to say loved, not loves."

She shrugged.

He tried to swallow the lump that had

formed in his throat. After three tries, he suc-ceeded. "I don't know what to say... just... thank you."

Amelie carefully moved the books from his lap and placed them on the bedside table. She climbed into his lap and ran her finger across his bottom lip. "I want you to promise me that you'll read these, Jack. You really need to read them."

He looked away. "I can't."

"What if I read them aloud to you?"

He looked back at her as though maybe he was really seeing *her* for the first time. He searched her eyes as he smoothed her hair away from her face. "Sounds like a good plan. Not now, though. Now... I need to give you your gift." He smirked, lowering her back onto the bed. She raised her eyebrows. "Yeah?"

"Yeah, but I should warn you this, um... gift is probably going to take a while."

"Those are always the best kind." She gig-gled. Jack kissed the tip of her nose, and she smiled. *There it is, that smile, he thought. God, that smile. So maybe he couldn't memorize eve-rything about her the way he'd hoped. But as long as he lived, he knew that he would never forget that smile.*

Jack lay awake that night, staring at the ceil-ing, thinking about how the tides had turned in their friendship. For as many years as he could remember, it had always been Amelie who wanted him. Amelie wanted to be friends. Amelie chased *him* around camp. Amelie followed him around like a lost puppy. Hell, just last summer, it was she who had begged him not to leave her. And now, he found it odd that it was he who needed to do the begging now. Jack knew himself though. He wouldn't do it. He couldn't ask her to stay. But there in the dead of night, when he was sure that no one was listening, he allowed himself one shot at it just so he'd know what it felt like. He rolled over, pulled her in close, and whispered in her ear… "Please don't go."

Three days later, Jack kissed Amelie goodbye in the airport terminal. "So you'll visit me this summer, right?" she asked excitedly as though maybe she weren't ripping his heart out.

He nodded. "Of course."

"And you'll read the letters?"

"Yeah… Probably."

Amelie didn't buy it. She pulled something from her carry-on… a pen, as it turned out. She grabbed his hand, turned his palm up to face her, and pushed the tip into it. "So, you should know that I've numbered them. There were two that I didn't open. One for your wedding day, and one for the day your first child is born." She shrugged.

"I don't know why, but I just couldn't. Anyway this is the one I think you should start with." He watched the pen move as she scribbled the number fourteen on his hand.

A voice overhead said something Jack hadn't paid attention to. She glanced down at the ticket sticking out of her bag and then up at the ceiling where the voice had come from. "Well. That's me. I gotta go…" she said stepping up on her tippy toes. She cupped his face and kissed his cheek, then his lips.

When Jack felt her pull away, he grabbed her wrist and pulled her back. He leaned down and kissed her softly. It took all he had to pull away. There were a few things in that moment Jack almost said. So he kissed her again, if for no other reason than to avoid letting them slip out. She smiled and pulled back. "Unfortunately, planes don't wait."

"No. They don't," he managed, as he let her go and watched her walk away.

"Hey, Amelie," he called before there was too much distance between the two of them for her to hear.

She turned back.

"Send me some pictures, would you, kid?"

She nodded and then smiled.

"Because I'm expecting that they'll be pretty damned good seeing how you have to go all the way to France to take them."

He thought maybe he saw her laugh, but he couldn't be sure. She looked toward the plane, then back and waved one last time as she handed the attendant her ticket.

Jack stuck his palm up in a half-hearted attempt to wave back. He felt his knees start to buckle as he watched her descend into the airplane. When he couldn't see her any longer, he sat down and stared at his hands. His mind was elsewhere until her handwriting caught his attention. *Oh, what the hell? He thought.* Jack pulled out the book and flipped to page fourteen. This day couldn't possibly get any shittier, he told himself.

My Dearest Jack,

If you're reading this, then you've probably just had your heartbroken for the first time. Or at least it feels that way, anyway. But I want you to remember, Jack, that this isn't the first time (nor will it likely be the last) that you've felt this way. You've been through so much already, and if you're reading my letter, then obviously, you've survived thus far. And while it may not feel like it just now, you'll survive this, too.

There are so many things I want to tell you

about love, Jack. Oh, how I wish I were there to tell you this in person, to hug you, and hold your hand. I'm guessing at this age, you might not like hand holding so much anymore, though. I try to picture you, what you look like now, where you are as you're reading this, and it brings me so much joy to think of you all grown up. I looked in on you tonight as I've done every night since the day you were born, and as I watched you sleep, I pictured the man you'll become. It's hard not to feel a little bit bitter knowing I won't be there to see it all. Oddly enough, though, it is with that sentiment that I want to tell you about love. If you are reading this and your heart is broken, you are lucky, Jack. I want you to pause a moment and let that really sink in. You are so damned lucky. Feeling this way, it means that you are living and more importantly—that you are loving. You cannot know how lucky you are to love until you've felt the immense pain of having to let that love go. It is a part of life. And as I am learning, it is also a part of death. Do not waste it, Jack. Do not play small. Lick your wounds, but then get back out there. Love harder next time. Most people don't do that, you see. They get hurt once, and they hide behind it. They use it to excuse themselves into living guarded lives, never quite feeling the passion, the love that they are capable of. But not you, son. Don't make that mistake. And I hope that if you consid-

er taking that route, you'll think of me and you'll feel my love and know that even though I may have lost my battle, that I didn't go down without a fight.

Neither will you, my love.

Neither will you.

I love you always,
Mom

P.S. Tips for healing a broken heart: time, above all else (don't worry, you won't feel this way forever), ice cream, and meaningful work. Now is the time to start a new project, Jack. Try something new, throw yourself into it, and let yourself get lost in it. You'll come out all right in the end. You always have.

ELEVEN

When Jack went back to school that semester, he did exactly as his mother had suggested and threw himself into his work. Early on, back in the fall, he started a poker ring, mostly to cure his boredom at first. He only later fully realized the extent of which he could earn a considerable living by charging his classmates for membership to this exclusive *"poker club."*

Jack, however, didn't stop there. He had newfound motivation upon his return. Even though he still maintained his soul-crushing day job, which consisted mostly of filing paperwork at a nearby investment firm, the price tag of his Ivy League education was no joke. And he refused to ask his father for money. Now, on top of that, he suddenly had a trip to France to fund.

One night, as Jack sat around the poker table, his mind wondered as it usually did to Amelie. He thought about where she might be, and what she might be doing at that moment. Devastated, lost in his own mind, and thinking of her, he realized he needed more. He needed to do as his mother suggested. He needed a new project to focus on.

It was at that moment, as he sat half-heartedly playing poker with guys who would no doubt be very successful in life, that it suddenly came to him. The vast majority of Princeton kids had the good fortune of their parent's money, and yet still had enough good sense to desire to make their own. As he watched them play week after week, he observed things about them. They were overachievers—hell-bent on succeeding at all costs.

So Jack took that notion and ran with it. He created The Harrison Group. Even though the group part was a facade, because it was really just Jack, it wouldn't stay that way for long. The Harrison Group was an investment firm where the members of his poker club could invest and double (even triple) their poker winnings in stocks. After two short months, Jack was running a business worth seven figures from his campus apartment. His father, had he known, Jack thought, would be really proud.

That summer in June, Jack flew to France where Amelie picked him up curbside at the airport in a borrowed car. She stood at the burn barefoot in a cotton dress. If Jack thought she'd been different any other time, the difference was magnified times a thousand this visit. For starters, her blonde hair was longer and *blonder.* Her skin tanner. Her mannerisms a bit more refined, more sophisticated. When he went in for a kiss, she surprised him by kissing both his cheeks. She messed with him by refusing to speak English, insisting they converse only in French.

"When in France." She laughed.

As they stood there outside the airport, he took it all in, and a part of him relaxed, maybe for the first time in months. Jack fell in love with her all over again in that moment. From the way the warm sunshine touched her bare shoulders to the way her bangs fell in her face to the way she shrugged as he reached over and tucked them behind her ear. He wanted to soak it all up. He wanted to soak her up. He wanted to get lost in this kind of happiness.

In the car, he reached for her hand, and she looked over and smiled. *There it was.* "I've missed you," he told her.

"Have you, now?" She winked.

The further on they drove, the more infinite Jack felt, as though he left every care he ever had back in the States. He was lighter, less worried. The south of France was different than he had imagined. More rural, perhaps. It was beautiful country, that he was sure of. Amelie was staying in a small village called Sault. To get there, they drove along roads that were set between fields and fields of lavender, which Amelie kept warning him that he should be mesmerized by. They were stunning and fragrant, but the only thing mesmerizing him in that moment was her. She went on and on rattling off facts about the area as though maybe she thought he'd come to see anything but her.

Finally, annoyed with his lack of enthusiasm, she pulled the car over on a quiet country road, put it in park, and climbed in his lap. She frowned at him, playfully slapping his hands away as he ran them up her thighs. He raised his brow in surprise when he realized she wasn't wearing underwear.

She shrugged. "I stopped wearing them. It's freeing really. Plus... it saves on laundry," she said, not taking her eyes from his as she unfastened his belt. Next, she went for the button and unzipped his pants. She reached in, causing a chill up his spine as she ran her fingers along the inside of his boxers, finally wrapping her hand around his shaft, pulling it free. "You want to do this *here*?" he asked, surveying their surroundings.

Amelie looked around and then back at him as though she wondered what the big deal was. "Uh huh," she said as she raised herself up and lowered down onto him. They made love there in the sun, in the passenger side of that borrowed car, on the side of the road, with the scent of lavender enveloping them. And Jack swore it was the best sex of his life.

Once they'd finished and composed themselves, they drove on at first making small talk, and then in silence. This was the thing about missing someone, Jack thought. You think you can't possibly miss them anymore... that your heart is about to burst from missing them so much. But the truth is that it's only after you meet again that you truly realize the magnitude of all that you've missed.

"There's something I need to tell you. Before we get there," she said, with a sense of hesitance in her voice.

He watched her face fall, and because he knew Amelie, he knew that whatever it was she was about to say, he wasn't going to like it.

She inhaled and exhaled slowly. "I'm sort of seeing someone. But... he's totally cool with you coming here. He knows all about you. About our... history, I mean, and he's fine with you and me."

Jack deadpanned. "What? Well, I'm *not* fucking cool with it. Why the hell did you invite me here, anyway? If you're with someone…?"

Amelie smirked as though he'd just said the silliest thing she had ever heard. "Everyone has multiple lovers here. And Mr. Serious… I invited you here because you're my friend, and I missed you."

God. She was hopeless. And that was it. Just like that, Jack decided then and there that he hated France. There would be other reasons he'd find later, but for now, he simply shifted in his seat and came to terms with his hatred. "So we're friends *now?* Well, then, let me ask you something… Do you fuck all your friends the way you did me, back there?"

Amelie pulled the car off to the side of the road and turned to him. "Oh, Jack… Come on! I knew you weren't going to like this… but *seriously,* can you please *not* make us *both* miserable? We have a week together. That's seven days, Jack." She brushed the back of her hand across his chin. *Her way of testing how angry he was, he figured.* "Can we please just make the most out of it?"

Jack thawed a little against his better judgment, but he wasn't about to show it. He crossed his arms, sat back in the seat, shook his head, and set his jaw. "When in France."

Amelie slapped his thigh. *Hard.* "That's the

spirit."

"So when do I finally get to meet the lucky guy?" He glowered, staring straight ahead.

She looked over and grinned. "Oh, Mr. Harrison... what am I going to do with you?" She winked and raised an eyebrow. "And you're so sure it's a guy I speak of, huh?

Of course, it turned out to be a goddamned guy. *Jack wasn't that lucky, he assured himself.* And not only was it a guy, it happened to be her fucking professor. Who, by the way, Jack wanted to strangle from the minute he'd laid eyes on him. For one thing, he was old. Sure, maybe he was talented and charming, according to what everyone *else* had to say, but whatever it was Amelie saw in him, Jack would never know. The other thing Jack didn't understand was why the guy was so damned friendly. It seemed as though he didn't have a care in the world. He was sleeping with Jack's girl, so as far as Jack was concerned, he thought he should have a lot of cares.

During his visit, Amelie took great pride in parading Jack around town, showing him off to her friends. Most mornings, they stayed in bed making love. Their afternoons consisted of bike rides through the hills and impromptu picnics wherever it was they happened to end up. Sometimes they simply drove to places Amelie insisted he see. In the evenings, they usually walked the cobblestone streets, wandering. He filled her in on the happenings at The Harrison Group and ideas he had for bringing on new partners. He told her about Princeton and his classes. She told him of Vincent, (the professor), and all that she was learning about. She explained the in's and out's of photography. She taught him a few techniques she used with her newest camera and yelled at him, calling him by name, when he refused to take any of it seriously. Even when she was annoyed, Jack felt a lump lodge firmly in his throat every time she said his name.

At night, there were the endless dinner parties. French people ate dinner surprisingly late, and a single dinner lasted for hours and hours. On Jack's third night, Amelie insisted they attend a dinner party thrown by the professor. Jack obliged but when he couldn't hack it any longer, he excused himself to the garden where the longer he sat, the more he wondered just why in the hell he'd come here. She wasn't coming home, he realized. Her life was here. His was there.

"Boo!" Amelie called as she practically tackled him from behind. "I've been looking all over for you."

Jack turned and looked her up and down. *She was so beautiful it hurt.*

"What are you doing out here."

He looked up at the midnight blue sky and sat down on the ledge. There were so many stars. He wasn't sure if he'd ever seen so many stars. "It's quiet out here."

She laughed, though just barely, then sat down beside him, and leaned her head on his shoulder. "That it is."

They sat in silence like that for a long while before Jack found the words he wanted to say. "I don't think I should have come... In fact, the more I think about it, the more I really wish I hadn't."

Amelie raised her head from his shoulder and shifted her body to face him. She crossed her legs underneath her and stared at her lap. "Yeah, I kind of figured as much."

"You've changed," he said without a hint of malice in his voice.

She looked up and met his gaze. "Have I? In what way, would you say?"

Jack sighed. "I don't know. You're just different."

"I really don't know what to say," she said and looked away.

"Why'd you come here? Why not come to the east coast like I'd asked. Or any other school back home?" Jack asked, though he wasn't sure if he really wanted to know or if he was simply trying to avoid any more silence between them.

Amelie inhaled. "This is where my dad came to study. I guess I just wanted to feel close to him somehow…"

Jack looked away, surprised and perhaps a little ashamed for hating a place so much that seemed so dear to her. "I hadn't realized that."

"Yeah. He came here to study poetry when he was around my age. It's hard to explain… but being here… it's almost as though I'm getting to know him in a way I might not otherwise. You know… considering."

He softened then, reached for her hand, and took it in his. "So… tell me about him. What have you learned…?"

She stared at their hands. "Well, sometimes I take his books, and I go to places I think he might have gone. I sit and read his poetry and wonder what he was feeling… what he was thinking when he wrote. And… I've interviewed some of the elders here, too. To see if they remember him… but so far… nothing. He told me once that I reminded him of this place. Of its beauty… He said that my name came to him here and that he knew if he ever had a daughter that he'd name her Amelie."

Jack squeezed her hand. "He was really lucky he did. I know he would be really proud of you, Amelie."

She sighed. "Yeah, I'd like to think so. But I'm not stupid, Jack. I know he ruined me for all other men."

Jack frowned. "How so?"

Amelie bit her lip and searched his eyes. "He adored me. He made me feel special. Everything I ever did was perfect in his eyes. And I know that as long as I live that no one will ever love me that way again." She laughed. "I mean, it would be a lot to ask. Don't you think?"

Jack cupped her face with his hands and kissed her softly. "I can love you like that. Just come home. Come back to the States with me, Amelie."

She kissed him back. "Oh, Jack. You know I can't."

He pulled away and searched her face. "You mean you won't. Not that you *can't*. Because that's bullshit. You absolutely can. There are plenty of schools back home. Is it *him*...? The professor. He's the reason, isn't he?"

Amelie rolled her eyes. "Vincent? God, no. He's just... Vincent. I like him... he's brilliant... but it's not like that."

"Then what is it like? What's keeping you here?" Jack pleaded.

"I don't know. It just feels like I've come home."

Jack stood and walked to the edge of the walkway and then turned away completely, unable to meet her eye. "I can't compete with that. Tell me how I'm supposed to compete with that…"

She stood and followed. "You can't. I'm glad you came. I wanted you to see. I thought maybe you'd understand once you were here."

Jack spoke, raising his voice more than he'd intended. "Understand! What the fuck is there to understand? I love you. I want to be with you and… you want to be here." He threw up his arms. "This… this place isn't me… in case you haven't noticed."

She lowered her voice and spoke sarcastically. "No, Jack. I hadn't noticed. Not at all."

"I can't stay here for another minute. I just can't do it. Quite frankly, what you're asking me to do is bullshit. I'm leaving tomorrow." He walked toward the gate without turning back.

"Where are you going?"

Jack kept walking. "To a hotel."

The following morning, Jack awoke to a knock at his door. He opened it to find Amelie standing there. She held up a paper sack and a Styrofoam cup and pushed past him. "I brought breakfast."

"How'd you find me?" he asked, running his fingers through his hair.

She sighed. "Small town. You're American."

Jack used the bathroom, and then splashed cold water on his face. When he came back out, Amelie was lying across the bed. "So you're leaving today, huh? You sure you can't be... um... persuaded otherwise?"

He frowned and pulled a shirt over his head. "Yes."

"Yes, I can persuade you. Or yes, you're sure?" She winked.

He glanced at his watch. "I have to be at the airport in three hours."

She stood and walked to him, slipping her hand inside his pajama pants. "Then I guess we don't have much time, do we? It's probably best to make the most of it..."

They drove to the airport in silence. Amelie white-knuckled the steering wheel as Jack pretended not to notice. He pressed his forehead against the cool glass, closed his eyes, and wished he were anywhere but where he was. *He couldn't wait to get the hell out of this place.* He ran through all the reasons in his head why he hated France and why he had to leave, *now.* Of all of the reasons he had, Jack realized the biggest was her. France was taking—or had taken, he corrected himself, Amelie away from him. It had made her worldly, and he knew, perhaps even from the moment she picked him up at the airport, that she could no longer picture a life back in The States. And with that came the realization, for Jack, that she couldn't picture a life with him, either.

"Hey, you," she finally said glancing briefly in his direction and then back at the road.

He opened his eyes to let her know he'd heard, and then shut them again.

She spoke slowly, softly. "Thank you for coming. I really am sorry about... everything. I know things didn't go quite like we expected... but you'll come back, right? Maybe... next summer?"

Jack squeezed his eyes shut noticing the burst of colors the tighter he squeezed. "No, Amelie. I'm not ever coming back."

She did a double take. "Like, ever? You're serious?"

"As a heart attack."

She patted his thigh. "I know you're angry with me, Jack. And I am sorry."

When he didn't respond, she let it go. As they drove on, each mile seemed to pull them further apart. Finally, she pulled the car up to the curb at the airport, and she turned and smiled at him. *Of course, leave it to Amelie to try to make the best of things, he thought.*

"I was thinking about coming home next

126

Christmas. We could go somewhere then."

Jack reached for the door handle and pushed himself forward. "I don't think so. Actually, I think… it's probably best if we leave things as they are, you know."

Amelie let out an audible gasp. She swallowed. "If you say so."

He opened the door and refused to let himself look back.

TWELVE

When Jack returned to school, he threw himself into work and women, which as it turns out may not have been the best plan he ever had. One night after a particularly disastrous binge on a girl from his economics class, he woke up, climbed out of bed and poured himself a drink. He wasn't much of a drinker. However, on this occasion, he allowed himself just one to dull the pain. His life was a mess, he told himself. From the outside looking in, Jack was successful. From afar, all probably appeared as it always did. He was neat, tidy, in control. He was on top of his game. But on the inside, Jack was one step away from crumbling. Leaving the south of France early seemed like a good idea at the time, but the further he got from that day, the more he regretted not staying. Three weeks had passed, and here he was, no more or less miserable than the day he'd left. That was the thing about Amelie— three days spent with her would always be better than none. Jack downed his drink and decided he needed to see her. He remembered the photo albums he had tucked away and figured if a photograph was all he could manage, then so be it. He went to his closet and pulled out the album she'd given him for Christmas in San Francisco. Jack paused when he noticed the second album there, and maybe it was the alcohol or maybe it was the loneliness, but he pulled it down, too. He ran his hand along the edges, opened to the first letter, and began reading.

Dearest Jack,

I asked your father to give you these letters. They're numbered in the order I thought might make the most sense. I'm going to trust that you'll find the right one at the right time. Which brings me to this one... I'm guessing you're reading this sometime just after my funeral. I can't tell you, baby, how strange it feels to type those words—but here we are, nonetheless. I know this is hard, Jack. I know you miss me, and with the rush of everything going on around you, the fact that I am really gone may not even seem real to you yet. I want you to know that I miss you, too, baby. I miss you so much. I'd like to think that you can still feel me there with you. It makes me happy to think that I can still comfort you somehow.

If I am wrong, and this does feel real, then I want to ask that you sit with that, Jack. I'm sure there are so many emotions that you're feeling right now—too many for a nine year old boy to understand. But you are smart, Jack. You have always been smart, and I know that you will figure this out. Please don't be angry, my love. Try to remember the good. Always remember the good. Though it may not seem that way now, we were so privileged to have had the time we did. It would never have been enough, no matter what... so it's important that you find the good in what you have. That's a lesson I want you to remember all your life.

I want to ask a favor of you, sweetheart. I want to ask that you please be kind to your father. I know he isn't easy to live with. But I also know that he loves you very much. He's lost in his own grief, and though it isn't an excuse for his behavior, there will come a day when I think you'll understand. And while that day will probably be a long time from now—the time will come when you'll love someone so much it'll make you question everything you thought to be true. It'll make you act in ways you couldn't have imagined, before. That's what love and grief do, you see. They are the extremes in this life. But they are also what really matter. Sit with that, son. Sit with the pain. Don't numb it out. Feel the feelings you need to feel, even if it takes time you don't want to take. The most important lessons you'll ever learn in this life are acceptance and forgiveness. It's love that teaches us those lessons, son. And with that, I want to ask that you forgive me, Jack. Forgive me for leaving. Forgive me for asking of you the things I've asked. I realize this was a lot to put on you. It was a lot to expect. I know this, and I just want to tell you how sorry I am.

Forgive your father, too, son. See the good in him, even when it seems hard to find. The truth about your dad is that he's not as strong as he appears from the outside. Lots of us are that way. Some of us are simply better at masking it than others.

I love you, Jack. And I'm still here when you need me. It may not feel like it right this second, but I'm here, in these letters, offering you the only thing I have left. And that is love. And above all else, it's acceptance. The truth about acceptance though, my love, is that you can not offer it to another if you haven't found it within yourself, and that is why I lied to your father about the medicine. It's why I asked you to do the same. I needed to accept that my death was inevitable just as much as I needed to help you accept it.

Feel the weight of it, Jack, and then when you're ready, release it. The things you need will always have a way of finding you, love. You just have to trust that it will be so.

I Love you always,
Mom

Jack closed the album, laid his head down on the desk, and cried himself to sleep.

Three weeks later, Jack was rounding the corner headed toward the business center when something familiar caught his eye. He walked closer, squinting as though maybe his eyes were deceiving him. Standing several feet away, smiling at him, was none other than Amelie.

Jack ran to her. "What in the world are you doing here?"

She toyed with her t-shirt nervously. "We didn't get a proper goodbye. And... I guess I just realized I was finished not getting proper goodbyes."

He frowned, and then hugged her so tight she coughed. *Damn it. As angry as he'd been, Jack never once considered how she might have felt when he left the way he had.* "I'm so glad you're here," Jack whispered over and over.

She pulled away slowly and searched his eyes. "Can we go somewhere and talk?"

He reached for her hand and led her to his

car. *His mother had been right. What you need always has a way of finding you.*

Jack tried to make up for lost time, he was so happy to see her that he couldn't keep his hands off her. Each time he attempted to make any headway, Amelie succeeded in brushing him off. She seemed distracted, off. He reached over again and pulled her toward him. She pulled away, her face draining of any color. "I'm pregnant," she said flatly.

Jack froze. His mouth went dry.

Amelie pulled her hair into a ponytail and continued. "I'm pretty sure it's yours. I mean... not a hundred percent sure or anything. But pretty sure... and I wanted you to know."

He put his hands over his face and rubbed at his eyes. "All right. Just let me think for a moment." He exhaled and then sucked in as much air as he could. "This... this isn't all bad. We can make this work."

Amelie sighed. "I'm not going to have the baby, Jack."

He swallowed. "What do you mean you're not going to have the baby?"

"I'm not going to have the baby. I have an appointment on Thursday... to get an abortion."

Jack felt his mouth drop. "What the fuck, Amelie?" He pointed toward her stomach. "That's my kid in there, and you're not even going to ask for my opinion on the matter?"

She looked away, out the passenger window.

"What in the hell did you come here for then?"

Amelie inhaled. By this point, she was crying. "I just wanted to see you. And I thought you should know..."

He threw up his hands, opened the door, and slammed it behind him. "You know what, Amelie? Fuck you!"

Later, after Jack had taken a walk and cooled down, he got back in the car and drove the two of them back to his apartment where they sat across from one another as if they were both daring the other to speak. A thousand thoughts ran through his mind. *Was he ready for this? What kind of father would he be? Nothing like his own, that was for sure. What would their baby look like? Like her, hopefully.*

"You don't have to do this," he finally said. "We could raise this baby together."

She grimaced. "You don't really realize what you're saying."

Jack stood, walked over, and kneeled on the floor in front of her. He took her hands in his. "Yes, I do."

She stared at their hands. "That's funny considering we're not even certain it's yours."

Jack lightly grabbed her chin and pulled it toward him, forcing her to look directly at his face. "I don't care."

She scoffed. "You say that now. But you have no idea…"

"I know that I love you. I know that I would love anything that's a part of you."

Amelie stared at his fingers as they traced the outline of her palm. "We both know that love isn't enough. I mean, haven't we learned anything here."

Jack released her hand and backed away. "That's bullshit and you know it! You don't want love to be enough, do you? It's you who doesn't want this baby, Amelie. Not me. Remember that"

"You're right. I don't want this baby. Or any other baby. I don't want kids. I really never have…"

He squeezed the bridge of his nose between his thumb and forefinger. "Well, I guess you should have considered that before. How did this happen, anyway? I thought you were on the pill?"

She straightened her back. "I was… I am. I guess I could've forgotten to take it a few times. I don't know, Jack. What do you want me to say?

Nothing's one hundred percent… you know that."

Jack pushed himself up off the floor and walked to the kitchen. "You wanna know what I know?" He pounded his fist on the counter. Jack felt the rage building, but he couldn't push it back down, even if he'd wanted to. "I know that you don't take shit seriously! You never have. This is all just a game to you! But you know what, Amelie? EVERYTHING isn't about YOU. This is my life we're talking about. This is our child's *life*. Why did you come here? Why not just take care of it in France? Why even tell me? How fucking selfish of you. I mean, you *had* to know what I was going to say…"

Amelie wiped the tears on her face with the back of her hand, and then met his gaze head on. "You want the truth, Jack? I came here because I didn't have anywhere else to go. Vincent dumped me, and I didn't want to go home and bother my mother with this because I didn't think I could handle seeing yet another look of disappointment on her face. I came here because I thought you were my friend. Because I can count on you. So, you can yell and scream… and pound your fists all you want. But don't think for one second I haven't already done all of those same things. You want someone to blame? Fine, blame me. I can take it. You think I don't already blame my-self enough, as it is? Do you *really* think this is easy for me? I know exactly what I'm doing.

137

You don't have to remind me. Because believe me, I'm aware. I'm killing my kid, Jack. And it's killing me. You act like this is all so simple. As though I'll just pop this baby out and live happily ever after. But it doesn't work like that. Do you have any idea how much having a baby will change my life? Every hope and every dream I've *ever* had will die, Jack. All of my career goals… gone. My life will *never* be my own again. And you're right. I am selfish. But at the same time, I want you to look around. Look around at everything you've worked so hard for and consider how it would feel if you knew it was all for nothing. Consider what it would feel like to give it all up. To just quit and for the next eighteen years, at the *very* least, focus all your attention on something else. The truth is that won't happen for you. It isn't the same. It will happen for me though. Having this baby would mean sacrificing myself. Because that's what motherhood is, Jack. Even in the best of circumstances, that's what it is. But please, by all means, tell me I'm wrong. Tell me I can still live the life I want to live. Tell me I can travel the world. Tell me that attaining my dream job as a travel photographer would still be within reach… and I'll say ok. I'll have this baby. I'll pay for my mistake. I'll have it for no other reason than because it's what you want. I'll have it because we both know it would be doing the right thing. Excuse me, though, for posing this question... the right thing for whom? "

Jack inhaled and slowly let it out. He didn't know a lot about kids. But he knew just enough to know that he couldn't honestly tell her what it was he so desperately wanted to say.

Jack and Amelie spent two days going back and forth over their situation but in the end, Jack realized she wasn't going to change her mind. The night before the appointment, which Jack knew would change it all, they lay in bed, backs to one another, careful not to touch. He was so angry with her, and even angrier with himself that he couldn't make her change her mind, and he worried that it would never be the same for the two of them. This was drawing a line in the sand, and it bothered him to think that they'd never recover once it was all said and done.

"I'm sorry, Jack," she whispered in the dark. "If I thought I could do it, I would. I know it doesn't make any difference, but I just want you to know that."

Jack spoke menacingly. Slowly. To make sure he really drilled it in. "If you do this, Amelie. That's it. I can't be a part of whatever this is anymore."

"I know." She sighed, her answer catching him off guard.

"And I can't be there tomorrow. I called a car service to pick you up and take you."

"Ok."

"So that's it... Ok? That's all you got? *That's* the best you can do?" Jack fumed.

Silent tears streamed down her face. "I'm sorry. Despite what you may think I really do wish I could be what it is you want me to be."

"Yeah, well, the girl I thought I knew, she was always a fighter. Oh, how far the mighty have fallen. Your dad would be so proud." *It was a low blow, he knew. But what choice did she leave him?*

She didn't say anything else. Instead, she simply gathered her things and walked out the front door. And just like all the times before—Jack let her go. This time though, he knew exactly whom his inaction was benefiting. It's always better to force ones hand where you could, and he knew that. It is, after all, hard to lose if you're not given a say in the matter.

The following morning, Jack paced his apartment. He expected her... hell, he'd wanted her to walk out. But what he hadn't planned for was what it was he would do once she did. Truth be told, he half expected that she'd come back, that she would change her mind. When she didn't turn up, Jack felt anxious. He couldn't let her go to that clinic alone, he realized. So when the car service he'd ordered showed up, he hitched a ride to the clinic. When he got there, he paced some more. No way could he go in that place. *What would he say? He'd say that he was here, that he wasn't a pussy, that's what he'd say.* He'd tell her that he didn't agree with what she was doing but that he wasn't going to leave her alone. That he held just as much responsibility for getting them there as she did.

Jack took a deep breath, opened the door, and scanned the waiting room. There was no sign of her.

"Can I help you?" a receptionist called from behind a glass window.

He looked from side to side. "Um…"

"Is there someone you're here to see, young man? Is there something I can help you with?" the lady asked firmly.

"Yes. Amelie. Amelie Rose. I think she has an appointment today."

"Is she expecting you?"

"Yes. I had to park the car," Jack lied.

The woman peered at him over her glasses, nodded, and scanned a file on her desk. "They've already called her back. You'll need to go through those doors over there. And to the right. The nurse will show you from there."

Jack felt the blood drain from his face. He gripped the counter. "Is she... has she already..."

The receptionist seemed unfazed by his question as though this sort of thing happened to guys like him every day. "No. They're just getting her worked up, now."

Jack swallowed hard.

"You'll hear the doors click as I buzz you in. Follow to the right."

A nurse met Jack at the doors and motioned for him to follow her down a long hall. She finally stopped, opening the door to a tiny room, which was lit by blinding florescent lights. The nurse motioned for him to go in. Amelie was dressed in a gown, her head in her hands, sitting atop an exam table, centered in the middle of the room. Jack had never seen a more sterile place in all his life. Not even with all the time he spent with his mother in and out of the doctor's offices and hospitals. This place was the worst of them all. *At least with cancer there's a chance, he thought. There was no chance in this place. What was done here, was done. It was final.* This thought made Jack want to pick her up and carry her out right then and there.

She looked up then. "Jack."

He noticed her eyes were swollen, like she'd been crying for a long, long time. "Please don't cry," he whispered, embracing her. "I'm here, now. And I'm so sorry," he said, as he gently rubbed her back and felt her tears soak through his shirt.

"I don't know what to say," she finally said when the sobs had subsided.

"Sometimes there isn't anything to say," Jack said, after he pulled back and wiped the rims of her eyelids softly with the pads of his thumbs. He brushed the hair away from her eyes.

She searched his face. "Thank you for coming."

Jack exhaled. "There's no way I could've *not* come. I shouldn't have pretended otherwise."

A nurse interrupted then. "Sir, it's time for us to take her back. You'll have to wait in the waiting room. I'll come and get you when we get her to recovery. It should be about forty-five minutes or so."

Jack panicked. "I can't go with her?"

The nurse glanced briefly at the chart then back at Jack. "No. I'm afraid not."

Amelie smiled just a little, for his benefit he knew. "I'll be fine."

He took a deep breath and reluctantly let go of her hand. "I love you, Amelie. I really, really do."

Her eyes welled up with tears, which Jack could tell she was trying her damnedest to hold back. She nodded. "I know."

There's nothing like sitting in a waiting room helpless to prove to one just how much they love another, Jack decided. As angry as he'd been, his anger had shifted a little now to something that more closely resembled remorse. In the fifty minutes that he would spend waiting to see for himself that she was ok, Jack realized that he'd been wrong. This experience hadn't drawn a line in the sand. But it had instead proved just how much you could possibly forgive someone for if you loved them enough.

THIRTEEN

In the days after 'the appointment', as Jack dubbed it, he cared for Amelie the best he knew how. He brought her food in bed. Food, which she didn't touch. He tried to make small talk to which she didn't respond. She'd sunk to a low that even Jack, as resourceful as he thought he was, couldn't seem to pull her from. She rotated between sleeping, crying, and staring blankly out the bedroom window. By the following Tuesday, Jack decided he needed to return to his summer classes, both for the benefit of his studies and his sanity. That morning, he went to class, and then headed to work in the afternoon after briefly stopping in to check on Amelie, who had been sleeping, still lying in the same spot she was in when he'd left that morning.

When Jack came home that evening and unlocked the door, he sensed right away that something was off. For starters, there no lights on in the place, Which could only mean one thing—Amelie still hadn't gotten out of bed. He headed straight to the bedroom. He was so furious by that point, partially at her, but mostly at himself for not knowing how to handle the situation. He turned on the bedside lamp only to find that she wasn't in the bed. He ran from room to room, looking for her before finding her lying on the bathroom floor facedown, in a pool of her own vomit. Jack pushed his fingers into her neck searching for a pulse. He watched her chest slowly rise and fall.

She was breathing. Thank god.

"Amelie? Amelie! What the fuck!" He picked up her head, dug the vomit from her mouth, and shook her. She rolled a little then and vomited all over his hands. "Amelie... Amelie. Wake up!" She stirred when he shouted her name but was otherwise unresponsive. Jack picked up the empty vodka bottle and tried to remember how much had been in it before.

Goddamn it.

He turned on the shower and let the water warm up. Then he placed her in the tub without bothering to remove the pajamas she was wearing. Under the water, she perked up a bit. "Amelie. Talk to me. How much did you drink? What did you take?" She shrugged, mumbled something he couldn't make out, and let her head fall against the side of the tub. He screamed her name a few more times. He shook her. Nothing.

146

Jack shut off the water. He wrapped a towel around her. *So she wouldn't be cold, he told himself.* And then he dialed 9-1-1.

It would be thirty-six arduous hours before they would allow Jack to see her again. He answered question after question from the authorities. Questions about how much she might have had to drink, what meds she was on, and how, as a minor, she had obtained the alcohol she'd consumed. Jack told them everything he knew, which it turned out wasn't much. He told them about the abortion and the prescriptions that the doctor had given her afterward. He gave them the information he had about her family and how they could reach her mother. When they determined he was no longer useful, they sent him to the waiting room where he waited, and then waited some more. He watched the clock as the minutes turned into hours and the hours into days. Jack had been asleep in the waiting room when he felt someone tapping his arm. He opened his eyes to find Amelie's mother standing over him.

"Fancy a walk?" she asked.

Jack stood up slowly and followed her out the emergency room doors. "How is she?" he demanded. "No one will tell me anything."

She pursed her lips. "I really wished you would have called me, Jack. What were you two thinking?"

"How is she?" he pleaded.

She frowned, and Jack couldn't help but notice how much Amelie favored her mother. "She's ok. Groggy. Tired. But ok..."

He exhaled all of the air in his lung and doubled over, resting his hands on his knees. "Oh, thank god. When can I see her?"

"Jack, tell me, how much do you know about my Amelie?"

"What do you mean?" he asked, confused by the question.

"My daughter is very sick. She needs treatment."

"What do you mean she's *sick*? What kind of treatment...?"

Her mother sighed. "This isn't the first time this has happened, son. Amelie has tried to kill herself before. She needs help. Serious help."

Jack backed away. "What are you trying to say? Amelie isn't crazy!"

She put her hand up as if to appease him. "Jack, my daughter is bi-polar."

He clenched his jaw and swallowed hard. "Bullshit. That's bullshit! She's just going through a rough time right now. That's all. She'll get through this. "

"Look. I know this is a lot for someone your

148

age to understand, but I need you to calm down, ok? Amelie is asking after you… but there's something I need to discuss with you first. Before I take you upstairs... "

Jack waited.

She hesitated before speaking. "I need you to be on my side about getting her help. Amelie cares a lot about you. She always has. Now… because of everything that's happened, I can technically place her in a treatment program without her consent. But the doctors and I all agree… we hope it doesn't have to come to that. The thing is, Jack… patients almost always do best when they make the decision themselves to seek treatment. So what I'm trying to say is… I need you to help my daughter come to that conclusion. I know it's a lot to ask. But Amelie looks up to you. And I really think she'll listen…"

He ran his fingers through his hair then shook his head. "Wait? Let me make sure I've gotten this straight. You want me to talk her into going to a mental institution? Because if that's what you're asking me to do… then you're the crazy one, lady…"

She stared at the ground before meeting his eyes as she spoke. "Listen. I'm going to let you see her. But I need you to at least consider my request. I'm not doing this for myself. I'm doing this for her. I don't want my daughter to end up dead. Certainly, you can understand that."

149

"Just let me see her now, please. I need to see her."

She sighed turned and motioned for Jack to follow her upstairs. It was the longest walk of his entire life.

Jack had not been prepared for what he was walking into. Seeing Amelie lying there like that with her arms in restraints did something to him that he felt he might never recover from. *She didn't deserve this*. He felt his rage building but tried his best to suppress it. He needed answers. *He needed to see her.* He needed to fix this.

He pulled a chair as close to the bed as he could, picked up her hand, and sat stroking it. He noticed the bags hanging from the IV line that ran to her arm. He inhaled the sterileness of the room, and all at once, so many memories came flooding back. Jack swallowed the lump in his throat and demanded answers. "What's wrong with her? Why is she like this? The abortion didn't cause this. I've done research." *He'd figured Amelie would be groggy, but not as she was now, completely out of it.* Comatose.

Amelie's mother poured a cup of water and pushed it in his direction. "For people with bipolar disorder, traumatic events... events such as having an abortion can cause real set backs. That… and we have no idea how long she'd been off her medication." He could hear the bitterness in her voice as she spoke.

"So you have her drugged up? Don't you think that after everything she's been through that *this* might be a little much?"

She smiled a guarded smile. "Sweetie. It's important that we take precautions to ensure that she doesn't hurt herself again."

"So you think drugging her up and locking her away is going help her? How is that?"

Her mother considered his question for a moment. She seemed flustered but calmed a little when she answered. "I know this must be very confusing for you. But you have to agree that *this* is better than how you found her in your apartment the other night. Amelie needs vigilance. She needs constant care right now. If you hadn't shown up when you did, Mr. Harrison, my daughter would be dead right now. So yes, I do think this is helping her. If it keeps her alive, it is helping. Anyway, I'll leave you two… I'll be in the cafeteria. Tell the nurses to have me paged if they need me."

Jack sat quietly for a few minutes as he thought his plan through. When he had it, he stood and climbed into the hospital bed next to her. He traced her face and kissed her lips. "I will not let them lock you up," he whispered.

Several hours later, sometime after the sun had set, Amelie began to stir. She opened her eyes and smiled weakly when she saw he was there.

"Hey," he smiled.

"Hey," she attempted, and then pointed at the pitcher of water on the bedside table. She raised her arms and sighed at the sight of the restraints. "They think I'm going somewhere," she managed. Jack placed the straw to her lips and watched her suck down the water. He refilled the cup two more times before she motioned that she'd had enough.

"This is ridiculous, Amelie," he said attempting to loosen one of her restraints.

She shook her head and pulled it away. "Better watch out. You're going to get us both into trouble."

"Yeah. Well, I think I've done enough of that already." He rubbed her forehead with the back of his hand. "God, I never should have left you alone."

"This isn't your fault, Jack." She looked around the room. "I did this."

"What I don't understand, though... is why."

"It's hard to explain... the pain, I guess. Sometimes... it's too much, and I just wanted it to go away."

"So you weren't trying to kill yourself, then. That's what I keep trying to tell them! But they

152

won't listen."

She smiled a little. "I don't know, Jack. I wouldn't exactly say that. The truth is… I just didn't care one way or the other. I'm just really sorry I put you in the middle of it all. I'm sorry you had to find me like that."

"Amelie. Listen to me. You are *not* crazy. No matter what they say. You know that, right? You're just going through a hard time, that's all."

She blinked back tears and eyed the restraints around her wrists. "Yeah. You could say that."

They laid there in silence for a long time before Amelie spoke again. "Jack."

"Yeah?" He recognized that tone.

"I don't want you to you see me like this anymore. I'm no good for you. I'm going to tell them that I'll go. I'm going to go to this place they're talking about sending me, and I need you to let me go. I need you to promise me… that you'll let me go without a fight."

Jack shifted in the bed. "You mean you want to go, then?" He narrowed his eyes. "I don't understand. You're not crazy. You're just sad. There's a difference. But around here… I don't know… it's like the twilight zone. No one listens."

She sighed. "I don't know what I want anymore, Jack. I just want to stop hurting everybody I love. I can't take the pity I see in your eyes. Or the disappointment in my mother's. Maybe I am sick. Maybe I'm not. All I know is that whatever this is… it's bigger than me. And I don't want to feel this way anymore."

He played with her fingers, unable to meet her eyes. "But… I don't know how to let you go, Amelie."

"I know you don't. You never did."

Jack looked up then. "What is that supposed to mean?"

"It means that I want you to let me go. For good, this time."

"Maybe you are fucking crazy. That's not gonna happen. I love you, Amelie." He snickered.

She turned to face him as best she could. "No. I'm serious. I've never caused anything but trouble for you. It's what I do. I find a way to destroy everything and everyone around me. And eventually, I'll destroy you, too. Just look at what I've managed to do already. I'm not taking you down with me, Jack. I'm not."

His gaze was fixed on her now. "That's bull-shit, and we both know it. This *is* life. It's not perfect. It is what it is. But you don't give up. You don't just give up."

"Sometimes, maybe you do. I don't love you the way you love me, Jack. Can't you see that?"

Amelie's mother appeared from behind the curtain. "Well, looky there. Sleeping Beauty's up. And guess what? I brought you some of your favorite things," she cheered, holding up a bag in each hand.

Jack looked back and forth between the two of them and realized what he needed to do. He glanced at his watch. "Visiting hours are almost up, so… I'm going to run. He kissed Amelie's cheek. He looked to her mother, cleared his throat, and walked toward the door. "I'll be back in the morning… In the meantime, see that she gets those things off her wrists, would you?"

He stopped just inside the doorway and nodded at Amelie. "See you in the morning, kid. I'll bring breakfast."

She smiled. *Even drugged up, in restraints on the psych floor, she was the most beautiful thing he'd ever seen.*

"I'll see you," she replied and winked.

Had Jack known then that was the last time he would see her for another two whole years, he probably would've said something a little more appropriate for the occasion. He probably would've stayed longer. Hell, he probably wouldn't have left at all.

PART TWO

Amelie

FOURTEEN

As Jack sat at the Princeton library pouring over anything and everything related to mental illness, specifically bi-polar disorder, somewhere across town, Amelie was having a conversation that would make it all for not. Jack had planned to bring in his own research to the table, his own resources, and experts on the subject. He'd intended to waltz into that hospital the following morning and prove that Amelie was not crazy, nor did she need or deserve to be locked up. Sure, she was passionate and moody. Free-spirited, he liked to call it. She was sad. But she wasn't crazy.

Back at the hospital, Amelie was busy doing some bargaining of her own. "Fine. I'll go. To-night, if it's what you want," she finally relented. "But only if you promise to give him something for me. There's something I need him to know."

"Something you need *who* to know, darling?" *Her mother had known exactly whom she was refereeing to.*

"Jack."

"Oh, honey, I thought we agreed on this. You need to let that boy go. You've said so yourself, he has a bright future ahead of him. And this kind of thing, well… it's just a lot for anyone to handle. Much less a boy of his age."

"I know, Mother. But there's something I forgot to say. Something I want him to know. So, you have to promise. Or I won't go." She held up the paperwork. "I won't sign these papers…"

Her mother waved her hands in the air. "Ok, dear. Whatever you want. Yes. Sure. I'll do it. I'll see to it that he gets your note."

Amelie pressed the pen to paper and signed her name on the dotted line. She set the pen down, did her best to compose herself, and then picked it up again and wrote to Jack. Three short paragraphs later, she prayed that she was able to convey enough to make him wait for her.

Dear Jack,

I'm sorry to have left with things in the state they're in. I'm sorry for it all, really. You certainly don't deserve the shit I've put you through, and I think somewhere deep down you must know that. But that's not why I'm writing, actually. I'm writing because I want to let you know that I lied. I do love you, Jack. I'm just sorry that it wasn't enough. That I can't be what you need. You de-

serve so much more. You deserve someone like yourself. Someone smart, someone strong, someone who hangs in there and fights for what it is they want. So that's what I'm going to try to be from here on out. A fighter. I'm going give this treatment thing everything I've got. I'm going to do it for you and for the child I never gave a chance. The truth is, I'm not sure that I deserve another chance, or that I even deserve to live, given what I've done. I know it doesn't make a lot of difference. No matter what I say or what I do, the outcome will still be the same. But hopefully, now the situation looks a little clearer on your end, and you can see that I'm not cut out to raise a child—that I can't even take care of myself. Hopefully, you understand that I never meant to hurt you. Sadly, though, I realize that's all I've done.

Because of that, Jack, because of the pain I saw in your eyes tonight, I've decided that it's no longer a choice for me to make. It's a given. I have to go. I need to get better. I need to be a fighter, for you. I want to make you proud the way you make me. I want to feel like I am worthy of your love. You inspire me to want to be better and without you, I don't know where I'd be. I guess what I'm trying to say is that you are my reason for trying. You always have been. I'm just sorry I lied about that before. But I want you to know it is the truth.

I hope you'll forgive me for leaving this way. I just couldn't take another goodbye. I couldn't let you beg me to stay. I hope that you'll write to me and that you know that I'll miss you so. Maybe when I get out, we can take a trip together. Until then, I'll focus on getting better. But no matter what, or where I am, I want you to know that my heart will always be somewhere with you.

Love,
Amelie

Unfortunately, for Jack, and for Amelie, her mother did not end up keeping the promise she'd made. It would be a very long time before Jack would read the words that Amelie had written that night.

Amelie's mother flew her back home to Texas where she had agreed to spend thirty days in an inpatient mental health program. Thirty days that quickly turned into sixty, and then into ninety. The inpatient facility felt more like a hospital than anything, and to say that Amelie despised being there would be an understatement. Her days were spent going from therapy to group therapy and back to her room again. Every day was the same, and they blended together until she found that she had to check the calendar on her therapist's desk in order to know which it was at all.

Sunday's were her favorite because Sunday was visiting day, and that was when her mother would come to see her. Amelie looked forward to those visits more than anything else. One cannot know how it feels to be cut off from the outside world, from everything you know, until suddenly you are. Nothing is familiar, and everything is empty. Mostly, though, she looked forward to her mother's visits, because that was when she would receive her mail. Her mother brought her letters sent from friends back at school in France and as well as from her grandparents. But it was always the letter that didn't come that she'd looked forward to most. As the weeks passed, and no word came from Jack, Amelie's mood grew darker and darker. She knew she really couldn't blame him though—after all, the last words she'd spoken to him were to tell him that she didn't feel the same way about him as he did her. She also knew he was probably angry about her leaving the way she did. Aside from all of that, she realized she had put him through a lot. Her letter had probably been *too* little, *too* late. In the following weeks, Amelie wrote two more letters, which her mother promised to send. After six weeks had passed with no response, she along with her therapist decided that it was probably in her best interest to let it go. They decided, in the interest of her recovery and release from the program, it was imperative she make progress. Unfortunately, it wasn't as easy for her to move forward as they'd all hoped— which is how thirty days ended up turning into ninety.

On day one, Amelie refused to take any form of medication, so it was given to her via injection, against her will. As time went on though, she learned to play the game. She observed that there was a system and that her only job was not to upset it. Once she learned to blend in, life there became more tolerable. Someday, she would upset the system, she told herself, but that day would not be today. *Defiance had a time and place, she knew.* Her one and only purpose at the time was to get out of there. By day fifteen, her medication had been transferred to pill form. Pills, which the nurses administered, watched her swallow and checked her mouth for afterward. It took her until day forty-two to master the art of the "hide and spit." This worked by using her tongue to push the pills up between her top teeth and cheek. She hid them there and then flushed them as soon as she was able. On the days when it didn't work, she forced herself to vomit the pills back up as soon as she could get to a restroom. It wasn't just that she hated the medication and the way it made her feel. Amelie knew she wasn't 'sick.' She refused to believe the diagnosis or the labels that she was given.

Around day sixty or so, the funk began to subside a little, and she found herself passing the days by getting to know her fellow 'inmates' as she liked to call them. She took photographs and wrote Jack letters she knew she would never send. And although she had gotten past thinking anything would ever be different between them—he was still the reason behind everything she did. She made him her reason for getting better. Her reason for getting out of there.

On day ninety, Amelie was cleared for release having exceeded every expectation her team of therapists had for her. She had managed to not only win over the physicians, but most her fellow patients, as well—serving as a mentor, a friend, and much later, a voice for those who often had none.

FIFTEEN

Amelie tossed and turned in her sleep. She thrashed about entangling herself in her covers before finally waking with a start, cold sweat pooled around her. Panicked, she shot up and rubbed at her eyes, and in a quick attempt to discern her surroundings, she began patting at whatever was within reach. Finally realizing where she was, which was back at home in her own bed, she slowly caught her breath, laid back down and tried to recall her dream and just what it was that had caused her heart to race, her head to swim.

"Tell me about your father," the male voice demanded.

The voice sounded an awful lot like her dad, only angrier, Amelie considered.

"What do you want to know?" she asked anxiously.

In the dream, she'd been back in the hospital lying on the couch in a doctor's office that resembled the room where she spent her days in therapy—only it wasn't.

"What was he like?" the voice insisted.

She raised her hand to speak only to find that she couldn't. Her arms were tied down. She struggled to get free.

"I'm waiting," the voice persisted.

"Take these off!" she pleaded as she inspected her wrists. "And I'll tell you whatever it is you want to know."

The booming voice laughed. "I'm afraid that's not how this sort of thing works, my darling."

Something, or more specifically, *someone* began stroking her head then, smoothing her hair. She'd attempted to shift upward in the direction of the voice in order to get a look at who might be touching her, but her head was too heavy for her to move. She swallowed back her fear and spoke quietly. "My father died. In a car accident. When I was seven."

The man's voice was rough when he spoke. "Ok. Tell me about him."

"I don't remember. Now, please take these off! I haven't done anything… I don't understand why I'm being restrained." Amelie cried.

"Surely you can recall *something*…" She felt the hand move down the side of her face and slide toward her shoulder. She did her best to move away, scooting a little, only it seemed there was nowhere to go. Her vision, and more importantly, her head felt too foggy to really give an escape much effort.

The hand moved further downward. "How does this feel?" the voice purred.

"STOP!" she screamed. "I don't like it!"

"My darling, don't you see? We're playing a little game here. The sooner you tell me what you remember, the sooner our session will be over."

Amelie spoke hurriedly. "He left for work one day... on a trip... he had a trip... and he never came back."

"Ok. What else?"

She thought hard, trying to recall something, *anything* that might make the voice happy. She hated the man with the booming voice, but she knew, despite the fog clouding her thoughts, that she had to get out of this room. "He... he used to tuck me in at night. I... I was the apple of his eye. His everything. That's what he used to tell me. He'd read me his poetry every night before bedtime... I think... whatever it was he was working on at the time. He told me about his travels. About where they were sending him next. I remember that whoever 'they' were... I knew I didn't like them because *they* kept sending him away."

"Go on," the man urged.

"When he was home, I was happy. My mom was nicer. Every night was the same. He would read to me, and then he'd kiss my forehead and

169

whisper my name. Amelie Rose, he'd say, and then he would smile. *I remember that I have his smile.* He'd say that my name was his greatest poetry. That I was the best thing he had ever done. That my heart was made of his and that it was better than gold."

"Anything else…"

Amelie felt the hot tears stain her cheeks as they poured from the sides of her eyes, but she was powerless to do anything about them. She felt the man's hand move upward and stroke her head once more. She shivered, but she didn't answer.

"How does it feel?" the voice prodded. "How does it feel not to be in control of oneself?"

"I don't understand what you mean," she said, her words slurring as she spoke.

"Miss Rose. There are only two kinds of people in this world. Those who are in control. And those who aren't. The more quickly one learns their power and more importantly, their position, the better off that person will be…"

Those words were the last thing Amelie could recall before she was jolted awake.

Amelie lay there that night, long after her dream and the panic had subsided, and tried her best to remember her father. The dream had unsettled her. Maybe she didn't think of him enough. She knew she'd always tried to honor him and his memory in one way or another. Even to this day, she still wanted to make him proud. But as the years passed, so did her memory of him. Her mother rarely spoke of him anymore and didn't seem to particularly like it when Amelie brought him up. Sometimes, Amelie would pour over old photographs of him and try to recall how he'd sounded, or what it felt like to be hugged by him, or try to picture what he might look like today. That was the thing she loved about photographs—it was what made taking them so important to her. Once captured, they were final. There was no end and no beginning. The pictures were it. They were all you had, your only portal into your past, and when your memory failed you, they simply became the memory.

Where her mother was all business, her father had been all heart. That's where she got it from, he used to tell her. There was a lot that she couldn't remember about him but what she did know was that life was never again the same once he was gone. Where her world had been full of color, all of a sudden, with his death, everything became black and white.

The Polaroid camera was the last gift he had given her before he left on the fateful trip of which he would never return. Just before dawn, Amelie forced herself out of bed and went to her closet. She still had the box the camera had come in. Sometimes, on days like this one when she missed him the most, she would take it out, turn it over in her hands, and picture the expression on his face when he'd given it to her. As she lowered the box down to eye level, she heard the familiar rattle of paper inside. It was then that she remembered the letters that she hid there.

Amelie had made herself extra copies of the letters Jack's mother had written just in case something had ever happened to Jack's. At the time, she assured herself that it was all in the name of safekeeping, but now she realized she did it for selfish reasons, too. The letters were achingly beautiful, and if she were in an honest mood, she'd tell you that she sometimes pretended they were written for her, and that it was her father who had left them for her. The letters gave him a voice when she could barely recall what his sounded like. In the quiet hours after dawn, she read the letters once again.

By this time, she'd memorized many of them by heart. But that morning, it was one letter in particular that stuck out among the rest. It was that letter which influenced her decision not to contact Jack. She realized then that she needed to let things be for a while. She needed to get herself together.

My Dearest Jack,

I want to talk to you about "failure" and letting go. From the time you were a baby, and even as a small boy now, I can see how willful and driven you are. Sometimes, I sit and watch you try to figure something out, and I marvel at the way you exhaust yourself. You refuse to give up, not even for sleep. These days I'm here to redirect your efforts when needed, to give you advice, to help you through the struggle. But as we both know, by the time you read this, that won't be the case. I can only imagine what kind of man you might be now, and it makes me so proud to think of you all grown up. I'm guessing that your determination and your persistence have served you well.

That said, I know your father probably won't be the one to tell you this, so it's important that I do. Failure is ok, Jack. Failure is necessary. I want you to understand that just as important as hanging in there and sticking it out sometimes, so is knowing when to let go. I hope that my death in some way has shown you that occasionally there simply is no other choice. Sometimes, your determination and persistence end up hurting not only yourself, but also those you love. I want you to know, my love, that it's all right to fail. You will survive and come out stronger and wiser for it. It's ok to say enough is enough and leave it be. In fact, not only is it ok, it's a necessity in life. You see, failure teaches us something. Failure is often a guidepost that turns us in another direction. It allows us to course correct. In my life, every time I thought I'd failed or I was rejected— it was only because something (or someone) better was waiting in the future—waiting for me to become the person I needed to be, to learn the lessons I needed to learn.

What I learned from failure is that everything good in life comes in its own time. You, my love, have never been the kind to accept that sentiment. Your way is to force things, to make them as you think they should be. And that's ok. But sometimes I want to ask that you don't. It's important that you learn to trust that inner voice of yours. I want you to understand that doubt means "don't." Don't answer the call. Don't rush to action. Let it be. Sit back and let it come to you. When you don't know what to do, be still. The answers, they will come. But you have to know when to take a step back. You have to know when to let go. That way, when whatever it is you've been waiting for shows up, you'll know it was meant to be. In the meantime, trust that what you put out will come back. It always does. This goes for hard work, money, energy, and most especially, love.

But you need to trust that it will, my love.

You have to let go and have faith. Nothing worth having ever comes easy. Which means that "failure" is a necessary part of success.

Remember that.

I love you always, and I'm so very proud of you.

Love,
Mom

It would be several years before Amelie would find meaning in the dream that had woken her in her bedroom that night and filled her with panic. In the meantime, she consoled herself with the notion that if there was anything good that came from her inpatient stay in a mental institution, it was that it had affirmed that she wasn't mentally ill, that she wasn't merely a diagnosis. She was simply someone who needed to learn to express her emotions in a healthy way.

Two weeks later, Amelie flew to Rome where she would spend the following year and nine months finishing her degree, earning a Bachelor of Science in Photography. Rome turned out to be everything she wanted and more. The city was a beautiful distraction from everything she so desperately needed to be distracted from. Where she thought she'd loved France—

Italy, it turns out was an illicit love affair. It was passionate, intense, and full of life. The country itself, she decided, was like her in many ways: defiant, intriguing, and a bit mysterious.

It was in Rome that Amelie found herself— where she came into her own, so to speak. She had the time of her life in a place where she was free to express herself, away from anyone who knew her. She was free to be who and what she was, and she felt more alive than she ever had. She spent her days studying and taking pictures. At night, she read and developed her art. On weekends, she traveled and ate and explored. She worked in cafes and took other odd jobs. She learned to sell her work. She had grand love affairs with Italian men and even a few women, here and there. But there wasn't a single day that went by when Jack didn't cross her mind at least once.

SIXTEEN

Four weeks before she was set to graduate, Amelie learned two things that would forever change the course of her life. One: she'd landed a job, her dream job, as Director of Photography at Travel Life Magazine. And two: a gallery in New Orleans wanted to show her work, but the caveat was that she was to be in attendance on opening day.

Five weeks later, she flew back to the States and then straight to NOLA. Amelie checked into her hotel, showered, dressed in her favorite little black dress, and headed to the gallery for the showing with ten minutes to spare before the event started. When she arrived, Amelie met with the gallery owner who showed her around. She was admittedly a little jet lagged and jittery, no doubt thanks to the two cappuccinos she'd consumed in the past hour. When the waiter appeared with a tray filled with champagne glasses, Amelie grabbed a flute and downed it.

The gallery owner, a man who appeared to be in his sixties, as far as she could guess, eyed her, amused. "We're very excited to show off your work. This subject is near and dear to my heart."

Amelie seemed surprised. "San Francisco?"

The man nodded. "I was born there. It was where my partner and I first met. It's where we fell in love." He smiled then continued. "When his work brought him out here, I followed."

"Ah. Lucky guy."

"I'm the lucky one, really. You'll see why soon enough." He scanned the room. "I'm pretty sure he's around here somewhere..."

Amelie eyed the photographs. "I'm a little taken aback seeing them hanging here." She let out a long sigh. "It seems like a lifetime ago that I took them."

The man nodded in recognition. When a waiter passed with a tray, he grabbed two flutes of champagne and handed her one, taking the empty one from her and handing it back to the waiter. He held his glass up, and then touched the rim of hers. "To San Francisco."

"To San Francisco," a deep voice whispered in her ear from behind.

Amelie dropped her glass and watched in slow motion as it hit the concrete floor below, shattering upon impact. She turned. "Jack."

The gallery owner took a step back. He

glanced back and forth between the two of them then stepped aside. "Excuse me for a moment while I grab someone to clean this up."

Amelie backed up and shifted her weight from foot to foot in an attempt to regain her balance. Jack reached for her forearm, settling her. He laughed just a little. "I'm sorry. I really didn't mean to startle you like that. The glass didn't get you, did it?"

She blinked and shook her head trying to reconcile what she was seeing.

"Here. Maybe you should sit," Jack said, leading her toward a barstool.

Amelie bit her lip. *God. He'd changed so much. His hair. It was dark, any trace of blonde now gone. And it was short. He was different… bigger than she remembered.* "What are you doing here?"

Jack stood beside her and surveyed the room. "I came to see your work. And my photos." He smiled. "Photos, which, by the way, I don't remember signing a release for."

She shrugged ruefully. "Sue me."

"Believe me, I'm considering it."

Jack reached over the bar, grabbed two glasses of champagne, and placed one in front of her. She picked it up and sipped slowly watching the crowd file past. "You look well," she finally offered.

"I am. And I could certainly say the same

179

about you." His eyes travel the length of her.

She seemed to consider what to say next, but then threw her head back and laughed as though he'd just said the funniest thing she'd ever heard. "Well, that's sort of a given, don't you think? The last time you saw me, I was partially sedated in a psych ward."

He stepped away from the bar and inspected the photograph hanging in front of them. He turned back to her and downed his glass of champagne. "Yeah. I'd say you've come a long way, kid."

Amelie glanced at the floor and then back at him. "You wanna get out of here?"

"You're the guest of honor. Don't you have to stay?"

She shrugged her shoulders and nodded slightly in recognition. "Give me twenty minutes, will you?"

Jack smiled. "They'll be the longest twenty minutes of my life."

Amelie led Jack by the hand through the lobby of The Hotel Monteleone when he suddenly stopped and stared at his shoes.

She looked him up and down, confused. "What are you doing?"

"Where are we going?" he asked, eyeing their surroundings nervously

"Where is it you want to go?"

Jack pulled his hand away and forced his hands into his pockets. "Um… how about the bar?"

She turned back, looked in briefly, and shook her head. "It's too crowded. And it spins. Let's try the one on the rooftop."

Jack put as much distance as possible between them in the elevator. He seemed to be relieved when the doors opened, and he followed her out to the rooftop. He ordered a bottle of champagne and sat facing her near the pool. "So what's new in your life? I'd heard through the grapevine that you were living abroad but not much else…"

She sipped her champagne then nodded. "Yep. Italy. Or Rome, if you want to be exact."

"Nice. Did you like it?"

"I loved it." Amelie exhaled. "It was… amazing. The people, the culture… the food."

"The men?"

She laughed. "Yes. Especially the men."

"So you're seeing someone, then?"

She shook her head slightly. "No. Not at the moment."

Jack pressed his lips together.

"What about you? What are you up to these days?" she asked, cocking her head to the side.

181

"Oh, you know… mostly more of the same. The Harrison Groups has expanded a little bit. We're in twelve cities now… and look to be in another five by the end of this year… so that's keeping me pretty busy."

"Just a little, huh." she teased. "Last I knew you were in one city." Amelie raised her brow. "You're living in Austin, I hear?"

"Yep. Downtown, actually. I can see now why you always loved it so."

She sighed. "Yeah. I haven't been back there lately. I hear it's grown a lot though."

"Growth is good for business, so I'm happy with it."

"I just accepted a job with Travel Life Magazine. They're one of the most widely read travel magazines in the world. Have you heard of 'em?"

He considered her question for a moment. "No, I don't believe I have." He swallowed the last of the champagne in his glass. "But I'll definitely be checking them out now." Jack refilled both of their glasses and held his up. "To new jobs, New Orleans, and growth. To us." She clinked her glass with his and took a sip.

There was a natural lull in the conversation. "Let's go for a swim," she urged, her voice low.

"But we don't have suits," Jack remarked.

"Who needs suits? You have underwear on, don't you?" She smiled, deviously. "It's practically the same thing…"

Jack pursed his lips. "You haven't changed one bit."

She raised her eyebrows, shrugged, and slipped out of her dress. "Perhaps… you should wait until I'm in my underwear before you decide that..."

But Jack was right. She hadn't changed a bit. He followed suit, removed his jeans, unbuttoned his shirt, and dove in.

It could've been the champagne or perhaps the fact that they were just so damned happy to see each other, but they giggled about everything and nothing all the way back to Amelie's room. At her door, Jack stopped and kissed her on the cheek. "I'll ring you for breakfast in the morning," he offered.

Amelie eyed him wistfully. "You're not coming in…?"

He stared at the floor. "Nah. I don't think so. I'm beat."

"Gotcha."

Jack hesitated, and then spoke, his voice sullen. "I'm glad I came, though. It's *really* good to see you."

She walked over to him and lightly ran her hand down his chest. "But you haven't come yet."

Maybe it was the jetlag, or the champagne, or the fact that he was half-dressed but Amelie decided right then and there that she wanted him. She grinned. "You're not getting off that easy, Jack Harrison." She raised one eyebrow suggestively and continued. "Unless, of course, you want to."

And just like that, he was on her, pushing her against the wall, he ran his hand up her thigh. "Key card?" Stunned, Amelie didn't move. "Key card, damn it," he ordered. "Give me the key card."

Amelie fumbled for it. Jack reached for her tiny clutch and took it from her, deftly fishing it out. "Ah, he said, holding up the key card. He opened the door and motioned her in before him. He let the door close behind them not taking his eyes off hers, and then took a step forward. She searched his face for a brief moment, her eyes lingering over his lips wondering how many unspoken words lie within them. Suddenly, Jack gripped her forearms and pushed her backward into the wall, hard. He tore at her panties, wrestled with his pants, and once satisfied, he searched her eyes for approval.

She nodded, and he thrust into her. Pressing his mouth to hers, he kissed her like she hadn't been kissed, well... ever. She tasted the familiar metallic taste of blood as he pulled away. He bit into her shoulder as he grabbed her hips and thrust forward. She matched pain with pain, as she dug her nails into his back. Jack groaned, and with one hand, he pinned her arms above her head and pressed his face into her neck as he thrust once more, and then slowed. Sixty seconds later, they found themselves in a messy heap on the floor.

"I don't understand how you could just leave like that," he finally said.

"I don't understand how *you* could just ignore my letters?" she hissed.

"I was… I *am* so fucking pissed at you, Amelie," Jack said. "Wait… what? What did you say?"

"My letters. You ignored them."

He shook his head. "I never received a single letter from you."

"Well, that explains a lot." She swallowed. And then she began laughing maniacally, only stopping when she could no longer breathe.

They made love twice more that night. Each time better than the last. No matter how many times or how many men Amelie had sex with, she had yet to find a lover who even came close to Jack. She laid there in the dark, listening to him sleep and tried to put her finger on what it was that made things between the two of them so intense.

The following morning, Amelie ordered room service for breakfast and sat sipping her coffee as she watched Jack sleep. When she'd finished, and he hadn't woken, she showered and dressed. She exited the bathroom to find him hurriedly ending a phone call.

He didn't look at her.

"I ordered food," she said motioning toward the cart.

"Thanks," he said as he stood and pulled the sheet around him. He headed for the restroom and closed the door.

Amelie sat on the bed and flipped through the hotel brochure. She watched from the corner of her eye as Jack emerged from the bathroom and dressed. She noticed the way he lifted the lid on the hot plate and picked at the food, seemingly uninspired. "Everything ok?" she asked nodding toward his cell phone.

He turned as though for the first time noticing that someone else was in the room. "Oh. Yeah… you know… business B.S."

He checked his watch and grimaced. It was after nine o'clock. "I haven't slept this late in years…"

Amelie stood and walked to him. "So… I was thinking… I'm not sure what your schedule is like… but they're sending me to Iceland for a few days… and I was wondering if maybe you'd like to come along…"

He started to respond then hesitated before finally saying, "I can't… there's too much going on at work…"

She placed her finger to his lips. "It's ok. No need to explain. There'll be other trips."

Jack backed away and sighed. The color drained from his face. "Sit down, Amelie. There's something I need to tell you…"

She didn't sit. She watched his face and waited.

Jack stared at the floor as he spoke. "I'm engaged. The wedding is in five weeks."

His words cut like a knife. "Oh. Wow." She scoffed when she could finally speak.

He glanced at her and held her gaze. "Yeah. I know."

She looked at the bed and then back at him to further dig in the point she knew was already weighing on him. "When were planning on telling me, Jack? I mean, we could've fucked a few more times before you sprang your impending marriage on me, don't you think?" she hissed.

"It's not like that. I never meant for it to happen this way."

She threw her hands up. "Really? What did you think would happen when you decided to show up here like this…?"

He rubbed his jaw and shook his head. "I

don't know. I guess I just wanted to see you and tell you in person."

"Well, you've seen me: check. You told me: check. So at least there's that," she said, through gritted teeth.

Jack sat on the bed and stared out the window. "Look, I'm sorry. I didn't mean to…"

Amelie sat down next to him on the bed. His remorse suddenly on full display, and sensing that he saw her as a mistake, she thawed a little. "It's ok," she interrupted. "It could be worse. I mean… you're not married yet, right?" she said, attempting a smile.

He pursed his lips. "It's not like that. I'm not like that… I love her."

She turned to him. For the first time in as long as she could remember, she came up with a plan on the spot. "I'm sure you do," she said, her mouth set in a hard line. "But I really think, Jack… that you should give some thought to coming to Iceland with me. One last trip. Just you and I. We don't… have to do this." She motioned toward the bed. "It's three days. Three days out of the whole rest of your life. That's all I'm asking. For old times sake. It'll be our last hurrah—only without the fuckery. Think about it… You're getting married. When are we ever going to have the chance to travel together again?"

He sighed. "We're not."

"Exactly."

188

He turned to face her. "Wait a minute… did you just say fuckery?"

She grinned. "I did."

"Jesus."

"So you'll think about it then?" she asked, nudging his arm.

"On one condition: that you'll come to the wedding."

Amelie sighed, and before she realized the full implication of what she was agreeing to, she added, "Of course. I wouldn't miss it for the world."

SEVENTEEN

Amelie shifted her position, leaned her head back against the seat, and closed her eyes before opening them again. It was turning out to be a bumpy flight, which wasn't helping her cause to try to get some sleep. She glanced at Jack, who, unlike her, didn't appear to be having any problems at all. All of a sudden, he reached out and grabbed her arm, startling her so that she let out a loud gasp and practically jumped out of her seat.

"What the hell?" she said, her voice hushed.

He grinned and eyed her suspiciously. "Can't sleep?"

"No. I'm worried about getting the shots they want. The editors weren't very specific, which makes it a little more difficult. I don't even know why they chose me for this job. I hate cold weather. Sometimes, I worry that I'm not cut out for this at all."

Jack considered her statement before he spoke. "Since when have you ever worried about getting a shot? That's not the girl I know."

She sighed. "Since they started paying me a lot of money to get them."

"So just pretend they aren't."

She shrugged and changed the subject. "What did you end up telling her?"

"Who? Elise?"

Amelie cocked her head to the side slightly and studied his expression.

Jack sucked a deep breath in and exhaled. "I told her I had some business that I needed to wrap up." He shrugged and continued. "No further explanation was required. Our relationship isn't really like that... we don't question one another."

She looked deep into his eyes, searching. "Well, I guess you didn't really lie then, did you?"

"No, I didn't," he stated, matter of factly.

"Does she know about me? I mean... does she know I exist?"

"She does."

Amelie nodded and closed her eyes. The next time she opened them they were making their descent into Keflavik. Noticing she was awake, Jack set down the newspaper he'd been reading, smiled, and pushed a small cup in her direction.

"Coffee?"

She stretched and took the cup from his hands. He turned his attention back to the newspaper. "So what's the plan?"

Amelie rubbed her eyes, and then cocked her head to the side. "Plan?"

"Photographers don't have plans?" he said, not looking up from the newspaper as he answered.

"Oh. You meant plan," she remarked sarcastically. "Well… we don't meet with our guide until tomorrow morning. So I figured that we could scout out a few locations today. Since they haven't really given specific instructions as to what they want… I figure I'll just take a bunch of shots and see what sticks."

Jack reached for her hand. She eyed her hand in his but didn't move to pull away.

"Sometimes… I pretend she's you. I know… that sounds crazy… and I don't mean it in a sick way or anything… I mean, it's not like I do it when we're having sex or anything, but it happens, just in general, you know."

Amelie stared straight past him into the aisle across from them and then out the window. "I'm no expert, Jack… but that doesn't sound very healthy."

He shook his head. "I don't know. I think a lot of people probably reminisce about their first love."

She looked back at him and held his gaze. "If you say so."

On the thirty-minute drive from the airport to their hotel in Rejinevik, Amelie stared out the window, mesmerized by the land around her. It was like nothing she had ever seen. There was dreariness to it, but hopefulness, as well. It was full of life, and it spoke to her, as though it made her feel every feeling she had welled up within. There was a paradox between its beauty and a sadness she couldn't put her finger on, something she couldn't yet touch.

Shifting in her seat, she closed her eyes as she let it wash over her. Suddenly, everything hit her at once. The shock of seeing Jack again, of learning that he was getting married, and the gravity of what this trip meant. Jack seemed to sense her unease and placed his hand on her thigh. The heat of his touch, the weight of it practically burned a hole right through her. She decided then and there she needed to figure something out and quick.

Once they checked into their hotel where Jack made sure, asking the clerk three times, that they be placed in separate rooms, they'd agreed to freshen up, unpack, and then meet in the restaurant downstairs. Amelie stepped out of the shower and was surprised to hear someone knocking at her door. Dripping wet, she wrapped

194

the hotel robe around her, went to the door, and peered out through the peephole. On the other side stood Jack, looking off down the hall, his hands shoved into his pockets. Amelie opened the door and stepped aside.

"I can't do this!" he belted out.

Amelie didn't say anything in response.

"I don't know how to pretend we're just friends. It's been a long time since we were *just* fucking friends."

She laughed against her better judgment. "Fucking friends… that's a good one."

"Amelie. This isn't a goddamned joke." He raised his voice as she watched the chiseled muscles in his jaw tighten, and then release. Finally, he threw up his hands. "We're here for three days, right?"

She narrowed her gaze, confused. "Three days, yes."

He nodded. "Then I have a proposal…"

Amelie rolled her eyes. "Proposing is what landed you in this mess in the first place, don't you think…" she said, cutting him off.

"Are you finished yet?" Jack asked, his voice stern and direct.

She shrugged.

He waited, and when she didn't retort, he added, "Good. Then I want to suggest that, for the next three days, we're just… us. No pretenses. Whatever happens, happens."

She wrung out her hair. "Ok."

The corners of his mouth turned up slowly. "That's it? That's all you have to say?"

"What is it you want me to say?"

Jack inhaled sharply. "I want to know that you're going to be ok. That we'll spend this time together, and then go back to our lives…"

"Like nothing happened," she said, cutting him off.

"Well, when you put it like that…"

Amelie crossed the room and stood directly in front of him. She took his chin in her hand and forced him to look at her. "Oh, Jack. There isn't any other way *to* put it. This is what it is. And if you're worried about me… well, don't be. I'm a big girl. I can handle myself."

Jack slipped his hands underneath her robe, his hands running along her breasts, finally cupping them. He squeezed gently as she watched his facial expression change, a mixture of relief and something else written across it. He let go, removed his hands, untied her robe, and watched it fall to the floor. Amelie took his hand and led him to the bed where they would stay for the next six hours.

When they finally did make it down to the

restaurant where they ate dinner instead of lunch, Amelie accused Jack of wasting her shower. "I reek of sex and… something else."

He laughed. "Whatever it is, it suits you."

"I'm starving," she said, glancing at her plate.

His eyes followed. "Clearly."

Amelie took another bite, chewed, and swallowed. "How's your sex life?"

He seemed surprised, to say the least. "Seriously?"

"Seriously."

Jack sipped his water and placed the glass back on the table. "It's fine. I mean… you know. We've been together for a while now, and we live together, so all of that stuff… it kind of changes."

She deadpanned. "Sounds thrilling."

"I don't mean it like that, really. It's good. Everything is good. But she and I… well, let's just say it's not like it is with us."

Amelie bit her lip. "How so?"

"Our relationship is different. Let's just leave it at that."

And leave it at that they did, finishing their dinner in silence. After dinner, they headed out on foot exploring the local shops surrounding the hotel and picking up much needed supplies Jack hadn't brought along. As they made their way back to the hotel to deposit the wares they'd purchased, Amelie broached the topic she'd been avoiding. "So... you never told me... is the wedding in Austin?"

Jack shook his head. "Hawaii. Her family has a place there."

"Nice."

"You know... your mom wrote you a letter for your wedding day. Have you read that one yet?"

"No."

"Yeah. Me, neither."

Jack stopped walking. "Wait... you've read them, recently?"

She faced him and dropped his hand. "Yeah. I have copies... and I read them from time to time."

He reached for her hand and led her to a grassy area just across from the shops. He sat and pulled her down, too. They watched a group of teenagers as one teenager grabbed another ones hat and played keep away within their group of friends. After several minutes, he looked at her and asked, "So, what do you think... of the letters? I guess I never considered that you might still have them, that you read them, too."

"I think they're beautiful." She smiled slightly. "There are a few I still have never read, though. The one for your wedding day and the one written for the day your first child is born, for example. I'm not sure why... I just never have. Maybe… it's because those seem more personal. Like they're a part of you that I'll never know. They've always seemed too far off, too far into the future."

After another stretch of silence, and more people watching, Jack spoke. "I don't know if I'm doing the right thing marrying her. I keep looking for a sign as though something's just going to materialize and wash away all of my doubts. I realize that I should be sure." His mouth formed a hard line. "Shouldn't I?" He finally asked his voice simultaneously pleading and forceful.

Amelie thought long and hard about how to answer, finally inhaling sharply. "I can't say for sure, Jack. I mean, yes, you do need to be sure. You absolutely do. But I think most people probably go into it a little nervous. Hence the term *cold feet."*

He smiled, but it didn't touch his eyes "Yeah, speaking of cold feet…" He stood, reached for her hands, and pulled her up.

Amelie leaned in, threw her arms around his neck, and hugged him with all of the strength she could muster. When she pulled back, she chuckled. "Who are you, anyway? The Jack I knew has always been so sure of himself." She grabbed his shoulders and shook him a little. "Must be love, if it's got *you,* of all people, feeling like this."

He searched her face as though he were trying to dig out every lie she had ever told. If it hadn't been so cold, and had they spent a moment longer standing there in that spot with him looking down at her like that, he might have just succeeded, she realized. A few seconds later, and she may have let slip what it was she really wanted to say.

That night, Jack called Amelie into the bathroom where he'd run a bubble bath. She eyed him suggestively when he motioned toward the tub.

"I'm probably going to go to hell for this, you know," he remarked as he slowly peeled her clothes off, took her by the hand, and lead her to the tub.

"For other things, I'm sure. But probably not for this…" she retorted.

He smiled, and walked to the vanity, placed his hands on the counter, and pressed his weight into them. He stood watching her reflection in the mirror. "Why didn't we ever get together? For real, I mean," he finally asked.

"You really want me to answer that?"

His eyes found hers in the mirror. "Yes. I do."

Amelie let herself sink further into the water until she was submerged up to her chin. "I don't know. I would guess it has to do with timing, mostly."

Jack unbuttoned his shirt, slipped out of his jeans, and climbed in the bathtub. He positioned himself behind her and leaned back, resting the back of her head on his chest. They sat there like that for a long time until their bodies were shriveled.

"If I didn't go through with it… if I don't marry her… do you think it could ever work between the two of us?"

Amelie knew exactly how she wanted to respond, but she wasn't sure whether to say it or not. "I don't know. But I don't think it's a fair question, really."

"Why not?" he asked.

She turned over and pressed her cheek to his chest. "Because your wedding is next month, Jack. Because you *are* marrying her."

"And if I didn't?"

"Don't," she said, pushing herself up abruptly. She grabbed a towel and wrapped herself in it. Jack stood and followed.

"Don't what?" he demanded. "So… we just aren't going to talk about it? How very typical of you, Amelie. Let's just pretend there isn't a hundred pound gorilla in the room," Jack spat.

Amelie sat on the edge of the bed and put her face in her hands. "Don't do this, Jack. Do not put this on me. It's bullshit, and you know it.

Why did you come to New Orleans? Honestly, why? I mean... to me, a man who is about to happily walk down the aisle doesn't just look up an old girlfriend and fly out to surprise her..."

Jack paced the length of the hotel room. "I told you the reason why, already. I wanted to see you."

"Then why not do it sooner? Why now?"

"You're the one who left in the middle of the night! I tried, Amelie. I begged you not to go. And you left anyway."

"I wrote you! You're the one who disappeared for two fucking years, Jack, That's on you."

"Yeah, well, we've already discussed that..." He pinched the bridge of his nose. "I didn't get your letters."

"You didn't think... not even once that maybe I needed you? Look at the condition I was in when you left... and then nothing..."

"You told me you didn't love me that night, Amelie. What was I supposed to do?"

"Oh, I don't know... how about be a fucking friend and find out where I was... how I was doing. How about *not* disappearing for two years! That would've been a good place to start!" she hissed.

Jack walked to her and kneeled on the floor below her. He rested his chin on her lap. "Amelie, I spent the whole night when I left the hospital going through every book I could find on mental illness. And the next morning, I took everything I'd found back to the hospital to prove those assholes wrong, that you weren't mentally ill. I tried. I did. But you left. You were gone. I called your mom. I called several inpatient hospitals... but no one would tell me anything, no one would give me any information. At the time, I thought I'd tried everything." He picked up his head and shrugged. "Looking back now, maybe I didn't. But what was I supposed to do?"

She ran her fingertips along the bottom of her eyelids wiping the tears that had spilled over. "I don't know. I just don't understand why you're doing this *now*. I was happy. I was fine. I'd gotten my life together... and then all of a sudden you show up and suddenly everything seems to be unraveling again."

"I know. And I'm sorry. But I needed to be sure. I couldn't walk down that isle and not be sure."

She deadpanned. "You should have been sure the moment you asked the question, Jack."

He nodded a sign of assent. "I thought I was."

"Then what's changed?" she asked half-heartedly.

"Everything."

203

The next morning, Amelie and Jack met their guide, a middle-aged man in the lobby. He glanced back and forth between them as though he couldn't believe the two half-asleep, apathetic creatures that stood before him could possibly be his charges. He checked his watch, ushered them toward the hotel entrance, speaking over his shoulder as he walked. "Better get to it, we've got a pretty full day."

First, the guide drove them to a small fishing boat, which they boarded for Videy Island where Amelie was to capture Videyjarstofa, which was known to be the oldest stone building in Iceland.

Upon arrival, she took several shots, which she seemed pretty satisfied with. She said she was ready to leave, but their guide insisted on taking a smoke break, so she and Jack agreed to explore a little and hiked the surrounding paths around the island.

"I'm going to do it," he uttered with confidence. "I've made up my mind, and I'm going through with it," Jack remarked, and then studied her face.

Amelie jabbed him hard in the stomach. "That's wonderful. Really, great news," she said, brushing past him.

"Hey. That hurt, damn it," he yelled after her.

She stopped and turned, her hands on her hips. "Yeah? Well, it was meant to."

They stopped briefly for lunch before traveling on to Strokkur where Amelie was to shoot several time-lapse shots of the Strokkur Geysir erupting. They drove on in silence, sitting at opposite ends of the backseat, putting as much space between one another as was physically possible.

For the remainder of their time, Jack watched Amelie work but did his best to keep his distance. He watched the crystal clear water pool at the surface, bubble, and then erupt. He marveled as it shot upward toward the murky blue sky and decided it was one of the most fascinating things he'd ever seen.

After an hour or so, Amelie appeared pleased with herself and motioned that it was time to go. He opened the car door for her and slid in beside her. He tread carefully as he spoke. "Get what you needed?"

She furrowed her brow and pursed her lips. "Always."

She was being coy, he knew. "How long does it typically take you on average to get a shot you're happy with?"

She turned her head and eyed him mischievously. "Oh… I got the shot I wanted within the first five minutes… the other fifty-five, I spent taking it all in."

"So it's gonna be like this, huh?"

She smiled, wryly. "I'm not sure I know

what you mean," she paused and held up her hands making quotations in the air, "when you say *like this.*"

Jack exhaled slowly. "I know you're angry with me about what I said earlier."

She didn't miss a beat. "And I know that you're trying to force my hand."

The guide eyed them in the rear view mirror. Amelie, with all of her misplaced anger, shot him a go to hell look at which point he promptly focused his gaze back on the road. "Force your hand? Force your hand to do what?" Jack scoffed. "I swear... that has to be the craziest thing I've ever heard."

Amelie leaned forward and peered at the driver. She spoke calmly, her voice giving nothing away. "Excuse me, sir. Can you please pull the car over?" The driver slowed and did as she asked. She yanked at the passenger door handle, got out, and slammed it behind her. Jack followed out the opposite door.

She lunged at him, but he dodged her by stepping back quickly. "Yes! Yes. I am fucking crazy. Is that what you want to hear? Well, guess what? I might be crazy, Jack Harrison, but you... YOU are full of shit."

He laughed, clearly amused, which only seemed to fuel her anger. "Oh, yeah?"

"Yeah. Fuck you, Jack. I am not... I *will* not let you put this on *me*," she spat. "I know what you're trying to do. And if you don't want to marry her, that's all you. I will not be the one to call the shots for you!"

"I'm not asking you to."

"Bullshit!" she screamed. "You want me to tell you not to marry her. Tell me that I'm wrong."

Jack rubbed his temples.

"Tell me I'm wrong, Jack. I want to hear you say it."

"You're not wrong." He relented. "Look, if you'll give me a chance... I'll explain." He looked around. "But not here, ok?"

She didn't budge. "Why not here?"

Jack looked at her as though she hadn't heard anything he'd just said. He pretended as though she hadn't just said the most ridiculous thing he'd ever heard.

He gestured around them and spoke very carefully, slowly. "Because we're in Iceland... on the side of the road... in the middle of fucking nowhere."

She stared at him in defiance. He smiled, opened the car door, and motioned toward the backseat with his hand. "Get in the car, Amelie."

She bit her lip and glanced from him to the car and back.

"Get in the goddamned car," he ordered.

"Please."

Reluctantly, she did as he asked.

The driver turned. "Lovers quarrels..." He

sighed. "Why must I always get stuck with your kind?" he mocked.

Amelie rolled her eyes. "We are not lovers."

Jack glared at her.

The driver pressed the gas pedal hard. He looked back and laughed. "The hell you're not, lady."

EIGHTEEN

Later that day, they took in an art museum, and then finally, what Amelie had been most looking forward to, The Blue Lagoon—one of the most visited places in all of Iceland. A man made lagoon, which had been turned into a spa that was fed by the water output from a nearby geothermal power plant. It was one of the most beautiful places she had ever seen, and Amelie continued taking pictures long after Jack had been in the water.

"You're coming in, right?" he called.

Amelie nodded, finally putting her equipment away. She stripped down and tiptoed into the water before inching back out a little. It was warmer than she'd expected.

"What time is it?" he asked as he wrapped his arms around her and pulled her in deeper.

"After midnight, I believe," she answered quietly.

"It's crazy how light it is. How it doesn't get

dark here..."

"Well, not in June, anyway."

He kissed her bare shoulder and dug his face into her neck. "I'm sorry about earlier. You know, it sounds crazy, but even the worst of times with you somehow still end up being the best times of my life. I really am glad I came."

"Oh, yeah?" She pulled back a little, smiled, and then playfully splashed water in his face.

"Yeah." He grabbed her before she could gauge his next move and pretended he was going to dunk her. Instead, he pulled back a little and tucked a piece of hair, which had strayed from her ponytail, behind her ear. "You're right. I did want to force your hand. But it isn't just for the reason you think..."

"It doesn't matter. Asking that of me for any reason is wrong. You have to see that."

"I do. Now, I do anyway. It's just that... well, I guess I wanted to know if you love me the way I love you. If you love me enough..."

Amelie let him pull her in closer. She wrapped her legs around his waist and traced her fingers along his back. "You... Jack Harrison... I could *never* love enough."

"But what does that even mean? What I'm asking, Amelie... is could you see yourself spending the rest of your life with me?"

She swallowed. "That's a lot to ask of a girl, you know."

He pulled away and looked directly at her. "A lot… or too much?"

Amelie bit her lip. "I haven't quite decided yet."

They next morning, they ordered breakfast in their room. It would be their final day together, and Amelie had just a few more venues to shoot—another museum and national park were on her agenda, both of which she hoped to get done early in the day.

After spending most of the night entangled in each other, they spent much of the morning in silence—it appeared that neither of them had much to say, but what they lacked in spoken word they made up for with tension. Amelie toyed with her eggs as her mind drifted back over the previous night. She thought about how Jack's hands felt on her body. The way all the best parts of him had fit so neatly with all the best parts of her. She thought about the way the words lingered on his lips as he whispered her name when he came. She recalled the low, smooth tone in his voice when he told her he'd love her forever as he simultaneously trailed kisses along her spine. She glanced up at him now, noting the way he gulped his coffee, and suddenly, found herself on the verge of exploding. She put her fork down, and swallowed hard, *too* furious to keep it all in any longer.

She picked up her glass and slammed it back down watching as the table shook and then her words spilled out. "What exactly is it that you want from me, Jack? How about we cut the shit, all right?" She picked up her glass once more and eyed him expectantly. "You're not one to shy away from saying what needs to be said... so let's have it."

Judging from his expression, she'd caught him off guard. "What do I want from you? That's what you're asking?"

She flicked the remnants of her toast on the plate. "Watch it, Jack. Repeating the question... *hmm*. Is this one of your sales tactics... is this your way of buying time?" Amelie felt foolish as soon as the words were out, but she was too angry to worry about making any sense.

He peered at her over his coffee cup. "I see you're in a pleasant mood this morning." He took a sip, and then cocked his head and raised one eyebrow. "Guess I didn't do my job well enough last night, eh?" He mocked, nodding at the bed. "Shall we give it another go?"

She stood up and pushed the chair, letting it tip forward against the table. "Fuck you."

"Ok... Ok. I'm sorry. Sit back down." He gazed out the window, his expression contemplative. "What do I want from you? Let's see…"

She eyed him suspiciously, but she didn't respond, nor did she sit back down.

Jack lowered his voice. "I… I want some sort of commitment. I don't know… I guess I just want you to tell me that things will be different. That it's possible for us to have a real relationship…"

She placed one hand on her hip. "And who decides what a real relationship is?"

"We do."

"Ok."

"Ok? Ok… what?" Jack asked, exasperated.

Amelie looked at him as though he had missed everything she'd just said. She sighed. "Ok, then. Let's decide…"

Later that night, after they'd made love twice more, Jack rolled over and lightly kissed the tip of her ear, waking her.

"I'm not going through with it. I'm going to tell her the wedding's off."

Amelie murmured something inaudible in recognition.

He shook her slightly. "Amelie? Did you hear what I said? I can't do it…"

Jack climbed over the top of her then, and

put his face as close to hers as possible. She opened her eyes. He searched them, waiting for a response. "Hello? Say something."

She thought for a second before responding. "Are you sure?"

"Yeah."

She inhaled then let it out slowly. "I'm sorry."

"It probably wouldn't have worked out anyway. The success rates on these sorts of things are fairly low. It's not a very smart investment, if you ask me," he said.

"Oh, Jack," she grunted.

He waved her off. "It's ok. Or at least it will be at some point."

"I know how much you love her. There's history there."

"Yes."

"Which means it's going to hurt like hell."

He exhaled. "Telling her, you mean? Yeah... I'm thinking we should go somewhere afterward. That it would help if I got away."

Amelie nodded slightly. "Sounds like a plan."

The following morning, they flew out of Iceland together hand in hand. They each had a layover in New York before catching separate connecting flights, Jack heading back to Texas and Amelie on to Florida for another shoot. They stood in the airport terminal saying their good-byes where Jack promised to call when it was done.

He kissed her once more, turned, and headed toward his gate when he heard Amelie call after him.

He looked back over his shoulder.

"Hey, Jack," she repeated as though maybe he'd missed it the first time.

He lifted his chin in the air to signal that he'd heard her.

"Where is it you want to go? Now, that I'm gainfully employed, I'll need to make plans."

He shrugged. "I don't know. I hadn't gotten past the somewhere with you part of the equation." He thought for a moment, and then winked. Surprise me, kid..."

She smiled and then handed the attendant her ticket and made her way down the ramp toward the plane.

NINETEEN

A week later, when the call Amelie had been so desperately waiting on still hadn't come, she told herself there had to be a good explanation. She alternated between worry and fury. A thousand reasons crossed her mind as to why Jack hadn't kept his promise. By day ten, she was so fed up that she hopped a plane bound for Austin—where she intended to find out for herself, once and for all, just what in the hell was going on.

Once home, the first stop Amelie made was to pay her mother a visit. Her mother put on a pot of tea as Amelie confronted her about the letters, about the real reason that her mother had placed her in the hospital, and why she'd lied for so many years. In the end, she did not get the answers she wanted, so she simply grabbed the letters and walked out. It would be a long time before she would speak to her mother again, and a very long time before they would be able to mend the relationship that had been so badly broken.

Her next stop was Jack's office. Amelie waltzed in and demanded to see him without bothering to call. If he hadn't given her the decency, why should she give it to him? Her intrusion wasn't received very well, and after being led to a small conference room, and told to wait, a young woman finally appeared and asked Amelie to follow her. She was led down a long corridor and showed into a second, more spacious conference room where Amelie was asked if she would like anything to drink. Amelie shook her head and thanked the young woman, very aware of the expression on her face clearly marked as *pity*. Whatever it was, it made Amelie's stomach turn. Approximately five minutes later, Jack appeared and was, needless to say, shocked as hell.

He closed the door behind him and crossed the room in two quick strides. "What in the hell are you doing here?"

She had been mistaken. It wasn't shock. It was anger.

"You didn't call."

Jack deadpanned. "So you flew all the way here?"

She motioned at her surroundings. "It certainly appears that way, doesn't it."

"Amelie, this... I mean... now really isn't a good time." He ran his fingers through his hair, stared at her, and then exhaled loudly. "I really wish you just hadn't shown up here like this..."

"You haven't told her. Have you?"

Jack lowered his voice. "Look... I can't discuss this here. Can we meet somewhere later?"

She took a few steps and stood directly in front of him, glaring into his eyes. He retreated. "Please, Amelie. I'm begging you... please keep it down. Let's not do this here, ok?"

"It's now or never, Jack. This is it."

He crossed his arms. "I'd like a chance to talk... to explain... but... like I told you, this is *not* the time or the place."

"Really? I'm pretty sure that somewhere within the past ten days or so, you could've found the time or place," she hissed. Amelie pulled out a chair and sat, propping her feet up on the table. She leaned back and met his eye. "I'm not leaving until you give me an answer."

He spoke carefully lowering his voice to a whisper. "She owns twenty-five percent of my company, Amelie. Which means that she pretty much has me by the balls."

"Surely, even *you* aren't ignorant enough to mix business with pleasure in such a way," she scoffed.

Jack frowned. "One would think."

Amelie rolled her eyes as the realization set in. "Jesus."

Jack stood for a moment considering how to

respond. Instead, he perched himself up on the table in front of her and folded his hands in his lap. "We were looking to expand, I needed capital... and her family offered. I thought I would be able to buy them out. But then we got involved, then engaged, and well..."

"So you thought you'd solve the issue by marrying her."

He laughed nervously, not exactly denying her accusation. "Well, it sure made getting a prenup out of her a whole lot easier. And hey, all is fair in love and war, as they say."

"It sounds like the two of you share the same philosophy on the subject, so I guess you deserve each other," she said, her voice cold, unemotional.

"What would you do... in my situation?"

She removed her legs from the table and scooted back in the chair, attempting to put as much distance as she could between the two of them. "What would I do? You want to know what *I* would do? Well, for one, I would hope that the person I wanted to spend the rest of my life with wanted the same thing for the same reasons. I sure as hell wouldn't force someone who didn't want to be with me to do so. *I* would walk away. But apparently, that's just me."

Jack frowned. "It's not that simple. I wish it were. But it's not. You'll see... someday."

Amelie stood and met his gaze head on.

"Well, then. I guess there is nothing more that needs to be said here." She took an envelope from her purse and handed it to him. "But I did want to give you these." He eyed the envelope, confused. "It's the letters I wrote to you while I was in the hospital. There are only a few of them. But I thought you might want them, nonetheless."

He swallowed and then tucked them into the inside pocket of his suit jacket.

She looked him up and down once more before she walked to the door and placed her hand on the handle. His voice stopped her from turning it. "Amelie," he paused before continuing, "I want you to know that I really am sorry." He stood and walked toward her. "You'll be all right, won't you?"

Amelie smiled. "Of course."

Jack put his hand on the door, keeping her from opening it. "I know it's really a lot to ask… but… I was wondering if you might still come to the wedding? I know what I'm asking seems ridiculous… it's just that… you're my oldest and dearest friend… and I've been thinking so much about my mom not being there and all… and I guess there's just no one who understands what that feels like the way you do."

Amelie swallowed hard, trying to dislodge the lump in her throat. He might as well have punched her in the gut. She took a deep breath and stared at the floor, willing herself not to cry.

When she thought she could finally speak, she did so slowly. Her voice broke, but she managed. "Sure. If it means that much to you, I'll be there."

"Thank you," he whispered, visibly relieved. "Oh, and Amelie…"

She glanced up briefly.

"Just so you don't think I'm a total ass… there's something else you should know."

"There always is…" she said.

"Elise is pregnant."

Amelie did a double take. *Another blow to the gut.* Feeling off balance, she leaned against the door to steady herself.

Jack reached her quickly, grabbing her elbow. "I swear to you… I didn't know before, I mean…" he said, his eyes pleading. She tugged her elbow away.

"You know what, Jack… it doesn't even matter," she said before she forced herself to open the door and walk out.

TWENTY

Jack shut his office door then slunk down at his desk. He rested his chin on his hand and gazed at the phone. He thought about picking it up and dialing her cell before changing his mind. He reached for the letter opener instead. Jack picked it up, hesitated, setting it back down before picking it up again. He sliced through the envelope, shook its contents free, and watched as the papers spilled out onto his desk. He picked up one of the folded notes and began to read.

Dear Jack,

I'm writing from the loony bin—literally. Ha! No, really, I'm here, in the insane asylum that is back at home in Austin, and I'm wondering why I haven't heard from you. It's been two weeks now and nothing. I'm sure you're busy at school, but I also pray that you're not too mad at me. Oh, and speaking of pray, yes, you read that right. I've taken up meditation here, which is a form of prayer in a sense, I guess. Anyway, it's the most amazingly intense thing. I can't begin to describe what it feels like to go inside your own head and look around—but that's exactly what it feels like. Like floating. Like you're an astronaut lost in the space of your own mind. It's freeing, so freeing. And quiet in a world that is anything but. Especially in this place. Now, I really do sound crazy, huh? At least I'm giving them good reason, and oh!—a run for their money. There's a lot more I'd like to say on that topic, but it's probably best not to put it in letterform. Even though I pretty much hate it here, I am feeling a lot better these days. I've almost come to terms with the abortion in a way. At least now, I am able to say the words, anyway. I know what I did was wrong, and I've since learned that even though it was wrong, what I was feeling was normal—a part of grief that comes along with it. I guess I just didn't feel like I deserved to feel grief or sadness or anything else, because well, it was my fault. I made the choice, after all. And so I tried to push it all down, to numb it out, and in the process, I caused a whole series of other problems. So, while I'm here, or for the remainder of my time anyway, I've decided to just feel. To let it be and deal with the emotions as they come.

Which brings me to you. I know I said it in

my previous letter, Jack, but I truly am just so sorry for everything. You have always been such a great friend to me, and I have done nothing but cause you misery. I realize that I'm not the easiest person to get along with, and well, I just want to thank you for always being a friend when I so desperately needed one. Obviously, there are other feelings there. I'll address those too, but first, I want to say how very grateful I am to you. No matter what, you've been my rock. You've always been the type of person I knew I could call on. That I could count on to be there for me. And I don't think our society gives enough credit for that. There is nothing more important in this world than having a friend, Jack. Nothing. I want you to know that no matter what, I will always do my best to be that for you. Maybe I haven't done the best job so far, and for that, I'm truly sorry. But from here on out, it's my promise to you that I will try to make you proud. I want you to know that it is thoughts of you that truly keep me going while I'm in here. Thoughts of the things we can do together, thoughts of the places we'll go, thoughts of being anywhere but here as long as it's somewhere with you. These are the things that keep me focused. Thoughts of you and of all the possibilities of what could be. So... I want to say thanks for that, too. Anyhow, I'd better sign off for now. It's time for "group." Remember how much you always love that at Camp Hope?

It's like a billion times worse in here. Anyway, bye for now.

Miss you tons and hope to hear from you soon.

In the meantime, here's to possibilities.

xoxo,
Amelie

Jack folded the letter, placed it on his desk and quickly typed an email before he could change his mind.

> To: Amelie Rose
> From: Jack Harrison
> Subject: Longstanding Friendships

Dear Amelie,

I'd like to apologize for the way things unfolded in my office today. Actually, I have a lot of apologizing to do regarding the way things have unfolded outside this office, as well.

Anyway, I don't really know what to say—other than, I'm sorry.

Forgive me,
Jack

Amelie flew in a day before the wedding and made sure to put as much space as possible between her and where the wedding party was staying. She fell in love with Hawaii from the get go. Knowing she would, she arrived with a list in hand of places she wanted to see and shoot, which is what she did right up until an hour before the ceremony. Having lost track of time, she was forced to race back to her hotel, to shower quickly, and throw minimal makeup on. She dressed in her finest silk dress, which happened to be black, of course, because, in her opinion, black seemed to fit the occasion.

She grabbed a taxi and arrived at the church with just fifteen minutes to spare. At the entrance, she straightened her back, tilted her chin, waltzed in, and took her place in a pew at the rear of the church. For two weeks, she'd dreamt of being the person who stood up and objected as the preacher asked if there were anyone who would like to object to the marriage, and all she could think of now was getting this over and done with. She planned to let herself be seen by Jack, congratulate him, and then bolt immediately following the ceremony. She took a deep breath, and then focused straight ahead before remembering that she hadn't silenced her cell phone. As she reached into her small purse, she felt a tap on her shoulder. "Are you Amelie Rose?" the man asked.

She nodded knowing exactly who this man was even though they'd never officially met. He stuck out his hand. "I'm Jack's father. He asked me to come for you. I believe he'd like a word before we get started."

"Oh, dear," she muttered before she could stop herself.

He nodded in recognition and took hold of her forearm. "Whatever you do, Miss Rose, I implore you not to let my son make a fool of himself and our entire family here today," he urged in a hushed voice, not quite a whisper, as he led her up the aisle and around to a hallway where doors lined both sides.

Jack's father stopped in front of one of the doors and turned to face her. Amelie felt her hand instinctively go to her throat. "Now, please hear what it is I'm about to tell you. I know that a fine young lady such as yourself can understand the gravity of what's happening here. Whether this marriage is right or not, or even whether or not Jack wants to go through with it—is not the question we should be asking ourselves at the moment." He looked from side to side before continuing. "The fact of the matter is that we're here. Along with three hundred other people— many of who have spent a great deal of time and money to be here today. People such as the bride's family, for instance. My son... is many things. But he is not a coward. Nor will I allow him to act like one."

Amelie stepped back and eyed the man from head to toe. The way she felt was written all over her face. "I beg your pardon. Your son happens to be one of the finest people I've ever had the pleasure of meeting. Now, if you'll excuse me." She turned, opened the door, and slipped inside.

Jack was sitting in a leather chair staring at something in his hands. He did not look up when she closed the door. Amelie slowly made her way to where he was sitting and lowered herself to the floor in front of him. She reached upward and grabbed the tip of his chin with her finger forcing him to look at her. "You wanted to see me?"

He eyed her cautiously and held her gaze for a moment before he spoke, his words slow and careful when he did. "They're all waiting, huh?"

She nodded slightly. "Let them wait. I've yet to attend a wedding that started on time..."

He handed what he'd been holding to her. She took the envelope. "From my mother. For my wedding day. Only I can't bring myself to open it... I thought... maybe..."

"I could read it for you," she said, finishing his sentence.

"Yeah." He didn't take his eyes off hers.

"But I also wanted to apologize in person."

She waved him off. "It's ok. Really."

He searched her eyes suspiciously. "Is it though?"

Tears filled her eyes then. She bit her lip. "It will be."

"I don't know if I can do this," he whispered, as a stray tear slid down his cheek.

Amelie leaned forward and wiped it with her thumb. "Yes. You can. You're going to be a daddy, Jack," she said, her tears spilling over. She smiled a little and wiped her nose on the back of her hand. "You know how much you've always wanted that."

He nodded. "I know."

"You're going to be fine."

"And you? How will you be?"

Amelie inhaled, and then let the breath out slowly. "Me? I'll be fine..."

Jack searched her face. "Amelie, I need you to be honest with me. No bullshit, all right?

Amelie thought about what he'd asked and paused for a second before answering. She willed herself to make this the most convincing lie she'd ever told. "You know, Jack, I've really given it a lot of thought... and the truth is it never would've worked between us anyhow. Even *if* things hadn't happened like they have. There's such disparity in what we want out of life right now. I have my life... and yours is here. You want a wife and children. You want to settle down. And let's just say that's not what I want. But look around you, Jack. You're getting everything you want here today."

"Not everything," he interrupted.

She looked at him with understanding and continued. "With us, there were always too many false starts. I believe that what's meant to be usually has a way of working out… and with us, it never did. Call it timing, call it fate, call it what you want. It is what it is. Sometimes in the end, the girl doesn't always get the boy—and that's ok. Life goes on. You know better than anyone that some love stories never get their happy ending… but it doesn't make them any less of a love story though, does it? It doesn't make the love the two shared any less relevant."

"No, it doesn't."

"So, you see, this is really all for the best," Amelie cheered, forcing a smile.

Jack glanced at his watch and reached out, touching the letter in her hands. "Will you read it? Please."

She drew a deep breath. "I'd be honored."

Amelie carefully opened the envelope, removed the letter, unfolded it, and began reading.

My Dearest Jack,

Wow. Here we are on your wedding day. I

have imagined this day so many times—starting from the day I found out I was pregnant with you. It's an occasion I guess every mother dreams about. And even though I can't be there in person to tell you myself, I want you to know that I am so over the moon happy for you today, on this day, the day you make the most important commitment of your life.

I'm sure that most mothers who write to their children on their wedding day probably give some sort of list telling them which steps to take (or not take) for a successful marriage, or some advice of that sort—but not me. I'm not going to give you the secrets to a long, lasting, happy marriage—after all, by now we know that I never got the chance to have one. But what I will say is this: love each other immensely— prepare for the "what ifs" in life but never stop taking it day by day. I think too many people get caught up in focusing on either what's happened in the past or what will happen in the future— without giving much thought to the present. Don't be one of them, Jack. Love your wife every single moment of the day. Stay focused on what's right in front of you, not what comes next—or what came before. Don't ever take her —or anything of it—for granted. Be grateful every day for the life you have and the love that you have found.

You are about to enter into one of the most meaningful relationships one can have as a hu-

man being. So make the most of it—not just to-day—but every day. Don't get complacent, think-ing "I Do" is somehow crossing the finish line—that the work stops there. "I Do" is merely the beginning of one of the most difficult and yet one of the most beautiful races that you will run in all your life. Cherish it. Work hard at it. Always re-member that it will be whatever you decide to make it.

Lastly, when the road gets rough, and it will—never forget the value of what it is you're fighting for. There is nothing more delightful in this world than knowing that there's someone out there who has your back, who is fighting the same battle you are fighting with you—and yet sometimes alone—but always for the same cause. And while there will be days where it doesn't seem as though this could possibly be the case, I want you to pause, breathe, and remember that beyond the hurt and the pain and the frustration, that there is a person in there who deep down really, really loves you. I want you to look at this person and remember that she is the same person who held all of the same wishes you're holding now, on this day—your wedding day. Come back to it from time to time, think back on where you're standing now, and remember all of the hopes and the dreams—the possibilities—that you two held today when you stood before each other and spoke your vows. Consider how far you've come and let that be a guide on the days, weeks, and perhaps even months, when it will feel like it's all too much. There will be days where it will seem like there is still so far to go. On those days, vow to wait it out—to enjoy your life together—taking it day by day. If you do that, then the mountains will seem like only hills. Hills are a lot easier to climb. And the view from the top is spectacular, I promise.

I love you so much, son, and I wish I could be there today to celebrate with you. But I want you to know that wherever I am—I'm smiling and raising a glass and toasting you and your new bride. I am so proud of you, son. Today and always.

I love you more than words could ever possibly convey.

Love always,
Mom

Amelie wiped her tear-stained face and tucked the letter back in its envelope. She wiped Jack's tears and hugged him tightly. They stood there that way for some time before there was a knock at the door. Amelie stepped back and looked at Jack. "It's show time. You ready?"

He raised his brow. "Something like that."

The knock grew louder. Then the door swung open, and with it, an audible gasp filled the room.

"Oh," Elise hissed as she looked from Jack to Amelie and back at him again. "Sorry to interrupt but we have guests waiting, Jack," she said, her words clipped, her voice lingering on his name.

"Elise, this is Amelie. Amelie, Elise."

Amelie nodded and knew that any sort of response she might offer wouldn't be well received. She understood that there was nothing to say in this situation, and so it was best not to say anything at all.

"Jack," Elise urged. He looked at Amelie and smiled. "Thank you, kid."

She returned his smile and watched as Jack walked to his bride, kissed her on the cheek, took her by the hand, and lead her out of that tiny tension filled room and down the aisle.

TWENTY-ONE

Summer 2012

Jack sat on the edge of his dock letting his feet dangle over into the water and watched the early morning sun reflect off the lake. This particular morning he did as he often did—just as his mother had suggested. He thought back on his wedding day. As of late, whenever he thought back to that day, there'd been too many times where he considered what might have happened if he had done things differently that day—specifically, if things hadn't happened in the sequence they had. But it was a dangerous game to play, he realized.

The wedding itself had been gorgeous, his bride stunning. No matter what happened, Jack would always look back on that day fondly. But at the same time, it would still also forever be a tad bittersweet. To his amazement, Amelie stayed true to her word and flew to Hawaii to attend the wedding, which even now made him question whether she had ever really loved him as he loved her. One thing was certain, though. Jack knew that if the tables had been turned that he would not have been able or the least bit willing to do what she did.

But where the wedding itself had been almost perfection, the honeymoon had been a complete and utter disaster. He thought back to his wedding night, and how while tucked away in their honeymoon suite, everything suddenly changed. He remembered how his world fell apart that night as the weight of what he'd done began to sink in. Jack tossed his fishing line into the water, reeled it in, and then cast his line again. He pictured Elise's face as he recalled the way he'd wrapped his arms around his new bride, how he'd slowly unbuttoned her wedding gown and carefully slipped her out of it. He recalled how excited he was to start their life together, how proud that the woman standing before him was going to be the mother of his children. He traced his fingers across her collarbone, and then motioned at the brand new wedding lingerie she was wearing. "Wow," he'd said.

Jack watched her eyes and noticed there was a look within them—the expression that she held, which in hindsight should have been his first clue on how things were about to unfold. "Not bad, Mrs. Harrison," he'd remarked as she wrapped her arms around his neck, leaned in close to his ear, and whispered, "Tell me, Jack… do you wish I were her?"

Jack pulled away. "Jesus! What are you talking about?"

"I think you know exactly what… if not *who* I'm talking about."

"Elise, don't do this. Come on. This is our wedding night…"

"And?" she said as she crossed the room.

"And… I was hoping to make love, not war."

She shook her head. "We're not *making love.*"

"Seriously? You are not doing this now. Please tell me we're not going through this tonight. And the answer is no, Elise. I do not wish that you were her or anyone else.

"That's bullshit. I saw the way you looked at her!"

Jack grabbed her then and pulled her close. He kissed her neck letting his hands trail down her stomach, which only seemed to intensify her fury.

"I said that we are not having sex. Damn it!" she screamed before crumbling to the floor. Jack stood in awe of how things had turned so suddenly wrong as he watched her become a sobbing heap on the floor, gasping between breaths. He knelt down in front of her. "Elise, honey, I'm sorry. But I swear. I'm telling you the truth."

"You want the truth, Jack?" she finally asked, once she'd managed to pull herself together a little.

He eyed her suspiciously and handed her a tissue.

"The truth is that we can't have sex because I'm bleeding. I lost the baby..."

Jack inhaled and paced the floor in front of them. "What?" He ran his fingers through his hair. "When?"

"Last week," she replied, her expression blank.

"Are you sure? Because I read that sometimes bleeding is normal in early pregnancy."

"Where? Where did you read that?"

Jack cocked his head to the side as a confused expression played across his face. "In the baby books I bought."

"Oh, Jack. How very typical of you. That's sweet. It really is... but yes, I'm sure. The doctor confirmed it."

He felt the color drain from his face. "Well, why didn't you tell me, then?"

"Oh... I don't know. Probably for the same reason that you didn't tell me about your little trip to Iceland. Or that your *friend* was coincidentally there at the same time. Do you think I'm stupid, Jack? All it takes is a tiny bit of research. And you really don't cover your tracks very well, love."

Jack sighed and sat down on the bed. He said nothing, which was his normal M.O. in times of trouble.

Elise crawled over to where he was sitting. "Look, Jacky…"

"Don't call me that. Don't you *ever* call me that!" he spat.

"Ok, JACK… You're right. Let's not do this tonight. I think it's best that we put this all behind us. I didn't want to ruin our wedding, so I didn't say anything before. Same as you, really. The doc says we can try again… that there was no reason for it… he said sometimes these things just happen."

"Is that why you threw the twenty-five percent shareholder bit in my face when I returned? Because you knew?"

"Oh, Jack. Don't be so dramatic. I wasn't exactly lying, was I?"

"Well, it sure makes a hell of a lot more sense now."

"Jack. Stop it. I thought you said we were going to put this all behind us."

"No. Actually, I didn't say that. I wouldn't even know where to start," he scoffed.

"Well, how about this? You lied. And I didn't exactly tell you the whole truth either… but what's done is done. It's time to think about our future now and let the past stay where it belongs, which is in the past. I promise to tell the whole truth from now on—so long as you promise to never see that girl again."

Had Jack heeded his mother's advice and taken his marriage day by day, he would've seen this for what it was. Instead, he'd been too busy thinking about what had taken place, and what it meant for his future. Unfortunately for Jack, like most people, he was too involved with his past and too concerned about his future to see what was happening right in front of him. If he had been paying attention to the present moment, he would've clearly seen that his marriage had been obtained under false pretenses and that by not consummating it, he could have quite easily obtained an annulment.

Jack dropped his towel and dove into the infinity edge pool as he did every evening at this time, rain or shine. He swam lap after lap until he was spent—until even one more lap became impossible. It helped clear his mind, he told himself. On this particular day, his mind drifted back to his wedding day and how he now realized that he was nothing more than just a stand in. *It could've been any groom up there at the altar that day, and it probably wouldn't have made any difference, he thought to himself.* But that's not to say that he didn't try. *By god, he had tried.* What most people didn't realize about Jack was that while he was a relentless businessman, he could also be forgiving—albeit he never forgot. That is exactly what he did when Elise confessed that she'd known about both the miscarriage and his trip with Amelie prior to their wedding. He forgave her. If he remembered correctly, "Let's just call it even" had been the exact words he'd used.

For the next five years, he'd tried so hard to make the marriage work. Jack didn't consider himself to be a quitter, so how it was that he found himself banned from his own home—banished to the lake house, and going on day forty-eight of this—he had no idea. Elise had thrown him out—or more accurately, pushed him out—and for the first time in a long time, Jack found himself without answers as to what to do about it. He didn't want to give up. He wanted to work at it. But working on a marriage takes two, and so far, he was minus one in that department. It baffled him. He'd given her everything she had ever wanted. With the exception of the one thing that obviously mattered most, and that happened to be one that even *he* couldn't fix—carrying a pregnancy to term.

Exhausted, Jack climbed out of the pool, toweled off, and picked up his cell. For the ninth time that day, he dialed Elise. This time was no different—his call went straight to voicemail. He set the phone down and sank back in the lawn chair. As he watched the setting sun sink further and further into the sky, he did his best to recall their last conversation word for word. He racked his brain trying to figure out what he might be missing—what it was that could have been so different from any other time that would make her act this way.

"We should just call this what it is," Elise said. She was sitting on their sofa resting her face in her hands. "It'll never happen, Jack. Don't you see? It *isn't* happening. It just isn't meant to be!"

"It's ok, sweetheart. We'll just do what the doc suggests and hire a surrogate," Jack said, as he leaned into her and rubbed her back in circles.

"No. I've already told you! How many times have I told you this? I do not want to watch another woman carry my child and know everything I'm missing. I just won't do it!"

Jack exhaled. "Ok, then. We'll just revisit adoption. I'll put a call into the attorney tomorrow."

She looked at him, disgusted. "I don't want someone else's child! I want our child."

Jack stood and paced their sparsely decorated living room. He couldn't for the life of him find anything in that room that reflected his taste. "Look, Elise, I know you're upset right now. I'm upset, too. But this is the eighth time now. And at some point, we have to start considering your health and the risks associated with recurrent miscarriages. I think it's time that we come to terms with the fact that we may be forced to pursue other options."

She glared at him, her mouth hanging open. "Upset? You think I'm upset? I'm devastated, Jack. Devastated! Do you have any idea what it feels like to have your body betray you like this? No. You don't. You don't have a fucking clue what it's like. You're little contribution to this whole mess just happens to be the fun part, doesn't it?"

"Elise. Please. I know what it's like to watch someone I love suffer. And I just don't want to do it anymore. We agreed the last time that we would try just once more. It's too risky. Even the doctors say so. I'm not just going to stand by and watch this happen again."

"Then what are you going to do, Jack?"

"Well, as I said… I was hoping that we could come to an agreement on our other options."

"As far as I'm concerned, there are no other options, Jack."

Jack stopped pacing and met her gaze head on. "Sure there are. You just need time. This is a lot to handle all at once."

"No. I don't think you understand. I'm finished. With the whole baby thing. With this marriage…"

"I know you're devastated Elise but please

don't say things you don't mean."

"But I do. Mean them. This is your chance, Jack. Run! Go be with her. It's what you've wanted all along, isn't it?'

He walked toward the front door. "I'm not doing this again, Elise."

"I'm not either. I'm done, Jack. You must think I'm an idiot. A fool! You think I haven't seen her photographs hanging on the wall in your office. You think I don't notice whenever a new one appears. Well, I'm not stupid, Jack! I know you're still in contact with her."

"We've been over and over this, Elise. And I've told you again and again I haven't spoken to her since the wedding."

"Do you know why I didn't tell you I'd lost the baby before the wedding? Because I knew. I knew that I'd lose you, and well, you know me… I like to win at all costs. It's why we've always been so good together. But the joke was on me with that one. I didn't win, Jack. Not really, anyway. Winning isn't winning when you realize you've already lost. Do you know what it's like to wake up next to your husband every day and know that he's in love with someone else? Do you have any idea how that feels? You've never been that good a liar, Jack. Tell me you don't still love her. I want to hear you say it."

"I love *you*."

"Wrong answer. Get out! Get out now! Just

go!" She shoved at his chest hard. Jack relented. She just needed some time to cool down and process everything, he assured himself. "Fine. I'll be at the lake house if you need me. I'll head back tomorrow afternoon."

"Don't bother," she said, slamming the door in his face.

The next morning, Jack was awakened to someone buzzing from the front gate asking to be let onto the property. It was a moving van, and it just so happened to be full of his stuff. Jack drove home the following day only to find that all of the locks had been changed. *She just needed time, he told himself.* She just needed time. He'd worked too hard and given up too much for this to be the end of it.

Three days later, a courier arrived with divorce papers, and Jack realized that no amount of time was going to change her mind. The following day, Jack met with his attorney in his office. Jack sat at his desk opposite the grey-haired man who rattled off facts, which Jack didn't hear. He was too focused on one of the photographs that hung on his wall. He looked from picture to picture before settling on one. It was sunrise in New Orleans. He hadn't remembered her taking that particular shot. He couldn't recall whether he'd been there or not when she did.

The attorney cleared his throat. "Beautiful photos you have here. Before we leave, remind me to get the artist's name. I'd like to purchase one like that for my wife," he said pointing to a shot of the beach that Jack knew had been taken in Hawaii.

"Will do." Jack nodded and focused his attention back on the man.

"So I assume the first question you have is how much the dissolution of your marriage is going to cost you. Thankfully for you, the prenup we had drawn up beforehand is pretty iron clad."

Jack tilted his head. "Actually, no. I wasn't thinking that."

The man took his glasses off and used his tie to wipe the lenses down. He readjusted them on his face and looked at Jack. "All right. Well..."

Jack glanced at a photograph of vibrant wildflowers and imagined how they must smell. *That picture was taken in Florence, he wanted to mention.* Instead, he looked at the paperwork in front of him. "I want to give her everything she's asking for."

The man frowned briefly before his expression turned to concern. "Are you sure? According to your prenuptial agreement, you don't owe her near what she's asking for..."

Jack waved the man off, interrupting him

mid-sentence. "It was all for her, anyway."

"And your business? Do want to give her the additional ten percent she's asking for."

"Yes."

"Mr. Harrison, as your attorney, I highly advise that you give this some more thought. There is no logical reason for you to give your estranged wife a penny more than what's listed in that agreement There were no children produced during the marriage, so I mean it when I say there's absolutely no reason for you to agree to any of her requests."

"You're right, there isn't."

The man stood. "So you'll give my advice some thought, then."

Jack pursed his lips. "No. I intend to sign today. I want to get this over with. There's no reason to drag it out. You see, David… May I call you David?" he asked pausing but not long enough to allow the man to answer. "I realize that what's in those papers means nothing to me. I've worked my whole adult life building all of this." He motioned around the room. "I've made many people very rich, and in the process, I've done quite well for myself. But you know what? Very few of those people are truly happy. All they care about is the bottom line. All they want is to obtain more, more, more. I've been thinking about this a lot lately. About what it is that I want, about what makes me happy. And there are only a few things on that list. One would be those photographs," he said pointing toward the wall. And the other is my place on the lake. The rest, well... the rest I really couldn't give a shit about."

The man nodded although his expression gave nothing away. Clearly, he thought Jack had lost his mind. "Ok, then, I'll have everything drawn up and sent over by close of business."

Jack stood and shook the man's hand. "Just so you know... I plan to sell the business once the divorce is final. Not that it really matters to me, but she'll actually get a whole lot less by agreeing to these terms than she would otherwise."

The attorney frowned. "I see."

"I just thought you should know that I haven't completely lost my mind."

"No. But whatever she has on you must be pretty substantial for you to be so generous."

Jack smiled and nodded in the direction of the door. "Guilt. Remorse. Regret. I've always found that they typically cost about the same."

TWENTY-TWO

Jack's secretary buzzed him. "Mr. Harrison, there's a Mr. McDowell here to see you. But I don't see him on your calendar, sir."

"It's ok. Send him in, please, Sherry."

The man entered Jack's office and sat before being asked. Jack had been told he was the best at what he did, but thus far, Jack hadn't been so sure. Even with the best private investigator, three weeks had passed and nothing. Not a trace of her. The magazine refused to give any information saying only that she was a contractor, and while they gave her a list of suggested shots and locales—they did not have the final say on when she visited each location. Sam McDowell, a man not much older than Jack himself, looked worn. He looked decades older, his eyes tired and downcast. Which could only mean one thing: no new information.

"So." Jack broke the silence. "Anything?"

The man pulled a folded set of paperwork

from his back pocket. "Nothing concrete. But I was able to locate an email address and pull a travel manifesto—places we believe her to be visiting in the next few weeks."

"Well, that's something," Jack said. "How'd you get the information? Maybe there's more where it came from."

The man looked at the paperwork before handing it over and smiled slightly. "Don't ask."

Jack read through the documents and glanced at the photographs. "South America, huh."

"Yeah. It's not a lot to go on. But I wanted you to have it, just so you understand that progress *is* being made. No matter how slow it may seem."

Jack looked at the paperwork and then back at the photographs. "I'm going to book a flight."

The man didn't look the least bit fazed. "Mr. Harrison, I'm not sure that is advisable at this point. We really don't have enough to go on—not enough in order to make it worth your time."

Jack smiled at the investigator. "Do you see all of those photographs, Mr. McDowell?" He pointed at the wall. "Every so often at random I receive the same padded envelope addressed to me here at my office. There's never a return address, but she always sends several photographs. Each one has a note on the back saying where it was taken. These photographs are her messages to me. They're clues as to where and how she is, to how she sees the world at any given time. But you'd have to know her to understand that. And if there's anything I know, it's Amelie and how she travels. I've travelled with her for over half of my life. So trust me when I say, I know a thing or two about her habits."

The man nodded. "But have you considered that perhaps Miss Rose doesn't want to be found—that perhaps this is the reason she never leaves a return address, the reason that her own mother can't tell us where she is?"

Jack rubbed at his chin. "I've considered that, yes. I just don't buy it. She's making herself difficult to find and yet, not impossible—hence the photographs. The thing about Amelie, Sam, is that you always have to work a little bit harder than you're comfortable with."

That afternoon, Jack sat down at his desk and composed an email to Amelie. He typed, deleted, typed, and then deleted some more before finally settling on this:

To: Amelie Rose
From: Jack Harrison
June 28, 2012

4:43 PM

Subject: Longstanding Friendships

Dear Amelie,

You're a hard one to track down, my friend. But word on the street has it that you might be traveling to Ecuador in the next few days. I find that to be quite coincidental as that's where I'm headed, as well. Anyway, I'd like to see you.

I'll be staying at the Hilton Colon Guayaquil. If you receive this in time, meet me in the hotel lobby on June 30th at 4:00 PM ECT. In the meantime, my phone number is below, and I'd love to hear from you.

Hope to see you soon, kid.

Jack

Two days later, Jack boarded a plane bound for Ecuador. He still had yet to receive a response back from Amelie, but something in his gut told him she would show, and if she didn't, well, he decided that he would still make a nice holiday out of it. It wasn't until he'd placed his bags in the overhead compartment and taken his seat that he began to have second thoughts. He fumbled with his phone and checked his email again when suddenly the lady in the window seat spoke up. "I see you're one of 'those.' My son is one of those, too. I just don't get it. Must be a generational thing…"

Jack glanced over at the woman, unsure if she'd been speaking to him. "Oh, don't mind me. I promise not to talk the whole time. But I just think it's so odd how people can be encapsulated in an aluminum cylinder, which happens to be shooting through the sky at a very high rate of speed and not even know the persons name they're sitting next to… Anyhow, I'm Jane."

He didn't buy it. He knew her type. She was a nervous flier, which meant two things for Jack: she'd talk the entire time, and it was going to be one hell of a long flight. He eyed the heavyset woman who appeared to be in her mid to late sixties and stuck out his hand. "Jack Harrison," he said before going back to his phone.

"I really have no idea what you kids do on those things."

Jack smiled but didn't look up. *Nip this in the bud now, he told himself.*

"I'm going to visit my son. He's a scientist. He's studying in the Galapagos."

Jack stared at his phone. "You must be proud."

She didn't miss a beat. "Oh, I am. Very

255

proud. But if you ask me, I think he's too focused on his work. He needs to find love, settle down, and give me a few grand babies. He seems to think he has all the time in the world. But when one gets to be my age... well, you start to see things a little differently."

Jack leaned his head back against the seat and closed his eyes. "I'm sure."

She didn't take the hint. "How about you? Do you have children? I see you're not wearing a wedding ring, but that doesn't mean anything these days."

Jack sighed. "No. No children for me."

To his surprise, the woman didn't respond right away. Jack felt the plane reverse and taxi down the runway. He checked his email once more and switched his phone to airplane mode. He felt the woman watching him from the corner of his eye. "This is my first time flying," she said and then paused. "It's hard to believe I'm sixty-eight years old, and I've never flown. I'd always meant to, you know. But somehow, life just has a way of passing you by."

"Yes. I do know," Jack remarked. He looked at the woman and considered that he was seeing her for the first time. He sensed her nervousness. "There's no need to worry, Miss. Flying is relatively safe. I've flown probably... hundreds of times and I'm still here. If you get nervous, just pretend you're somewhere else. That's what most people do."

The lady smiled. "Hundreds of times? It sounds like you're well-traveled. Care to humor an old woman and tell me about the places you've visited? It really helps my nerves to focus on conversation. "

Jack remembered his mother making the same request during her chemo treatments, and especially in her final days. *Talk to me, she'd say. Tell me about your day. Tell me about the weather. Tell me about school.* Jack would spend hours talking, telling her about everything and nothing. He'd forgotten about that until now. He swallowed hard. And then he spent the next five hours telling a random stranger his life story.

"This friend you're going to see," the woman smiled, "she sounds really special."

Jack nodded. "She is."

"Do you think she'll show?"

He pondered the question for a moment. "You know, I really don't know. We've been through so much together that I'd like to think that if she's received my correspondence, she will, but then again, I know I really hurt her. And who knows, maybe she's happily married with a few children by now. Maybe she has no desire to see me, to revisit the past."

"For what it's worth, dear, I think you're doing the right thing, flying out here. So many people would call or write or email, as you young people like to do, and leave it at that—but not you. You're actually showing up. And showing up is what matters in life. It makes all the difference. Even if the outcome isn't what you might've hoped for. No matter what... at least you'll always have that."

Jack checked into his hotel with three hours to spare before the time he'd proposed to Amelie that they meet in the lobby. He went upstairs, showered, unpacked and dressed in a clean pair of blue jeans and a button down shirt. He paced the room for a bit, and then powered up his laptop, checked his email, fumbled around the room a bit longer before deciding to head down to the bar to kill some time. Jack ordered a glass of red wine and drank half. He checked his watch repeatedly until finally, with half an hour remaining, he made his way out into the lobby to wait. Jack heard the familiar voice call his name as soon as he rounded the corner. He looked up to see Amelie barreling toward him. He braced himself as she crashed into him, catching him a little off guard when she jumped into his arms and wrapped her legs around his waist. He tripped backward a bit before he was to able steady himself by evening out her weight. He regained his balance and pulled back a little trying to see her face. She wrapped her arms around his neck and dug her face into his neck. "Amelie. I can't breathe." He reached up and attempted to loosen the grip she had around his neck. "Hey. Hey!" he whispered. "You're cutting off my air supply…"

She pulled back then and let her legs drop to the floor. "I can't believe you're really here!"

Jack looked confused. "Didn't you get my email?"

Amelie eyed him up and down. "Yeah. Why?"

"Because you didn't respond."

She waved her hand in the air as though she were dismissing his concern. "I wanted to surprise you."

Jack smiled and took her in. She was beautiful—her blonde hair piled in a messy bun that sat atop her head, her face bare without a trace of makeup, and she was dressed casually in shorts, a tank top, and flip-flops. *Not much had changed, Jack thought.* He shook his head. "Yeah, well, a response would've surprised me. I never have— ever understood your logic."

"When did you get in? Are you hungry? I'm

starving… and I know just the place," she asked as she grabbed his hand and pulled him toward the exit.

"Amelie." Jack stopped mid-stride.

She turned and waited.

"It's really, really good to see you."

Amelie led him into a poorly lit crowded restaurant. She nodded to a waiter who appeared and said something in Spanish that Jack wasn't quick enough to catch. He glanced around the place and back at Amelie. "You're sure you want to eat in this place… it doesn't look very safe."

She laughed. "I consider this to be one of the finest eateries in all of South America. And believe me when I say I've tried quite a few of them"

The waiter set two bottled waters down at their table. Jack picked up one of them, twisted the cap off, and pushed it in her direction. He did the same to his and took a sip. "So you come here often? To South America, I mean?"

She nodded. "Yeah. Actually, I live here part of the time, when I'm not traveling so much." She gulped her water and twisted the cap back on. "But what about you? What brings you here? Business? Pleasure?"

260

"You."

She furrowed her brow. "Me?"

"I wanted to see you."

"Oh." She swallowed. Amelie paused and picked at the label on her bottle of water. "I heard about the divorce. I'm sorry…"

Jack eyed her, confused. "You did? How?"

Amelie smiled wryly. "Google alerts."

"Ah. So you've been stalking me, then."

"I prefer to call it keeping tabs on an old friend…"

He nodded in her direction. "What about you? What've you been up to?" He glanced at her ring finger though he'd already noted it was bare.

"Work mostly. But I have three kids and a very handsome husband. They keep me pretty busy."

Jack felt his mouth go dry. "Oh, wow. The kids… what are their ages?"

She threw her head back and laughed. "Geez, Jack, relax. I'm just messing with you. No kids for me. No husband, either." She couldn't stop giggling. "I'm sorry. That was mean, I know. But you're practically as white as a ghost."

He frowned. "That was mean."

The waiter placed two plates on the table then and walked away. "I ordered you the special. I hope that's ok."

He shrugged, nonchalantly. "Are you seeing

anyone?"

Amelie stabbed at her food and took a bite. "You don't waste any time, do you?"

Jack looked away.

She caught herself. "Oh... no... I didn't mean it like that. I just meant... that you're full of questions, that's all." She slid her hand across the table and placed it on top of his. "Jack, I'm sorry. I didn't mean to offend you."

He looked back at her and grinned. "Ha! No offense taken. That was me getting you back. And forcing you to touch me." He winked. "I'm good like that."

She slapped his hand. "Nice one. I should've known you, Jack Harrison, lack the feelings most of us humans carry around."

"I do not."

Amelie started to speak, but then hesitated and looked away before turning back. When she spoke, her tone had changed. "I am seeing someone, actually."

Jack treaded carefully just to make sure she wasn't joking again. "Can't say I'm surprised. I mean look at you... you're stunning."

She smiled slightly. "I'm really glad you're here. There's so much I want to show you."

He reached for her hand her eyes immediately followed his hand as it brushed hers. "That's good. Because there's so much I want to see."

After they had eaten, Amelie insisted they should head off to one of the National Parks. There was something she wanted to shoot when the lighting was right, and she wanted him to come along. Jack informed her that he needed to stop back at the hotel to change his clothes and his shoes, which is how with luck and a little charm they ended up back in his room.

Amelie sat on the bed and watched him as he fumbled through one of his suitcases. She nodded toward the other one. "I'm surprised you brought two of them. I've never seen you travel with two before."

He shrugged. "Maybe I plan on staying a while."

She threw her head back and laughed. "Right."

Jack pretended to ignore her laughter and continued searching for the item of clothing he wanted to wear. "Why? Would that be such a bad thing?"

She looked up and met his gaze. "You're serious?"

He backtracked a little. "Well, yeah. Sort of."

"But what about your work?"

"I'm selling The Harrison Group."

"What? No! Why?" She was so taken aback

by what he'd said that she couldn't find the right words with which to respond.

He shrugged slightly. "My heart just wasn't in it anymore."

"Since when have you ever cared about that?" she asked, her voice uneven.

He looked toward the balcony door and then back at her. "Since I decided not to settle any longer. I want something that lights me up. Something that makes me excited to wake up. I don't really need to work. At least not for a while, anyway. I've done pretty well for myself. So I figure that I'll travel around for a bit until something strikes my fancy."

She furrowed her brow then smiled. "Who are you, and what have you done with Jack Harrison."

He laughed. "It's me. I'm him. Just a little wiser, that's all." He gave up on what he'd been looking for and sat down on the bed beside her. "The thing is, for so long I had my life all mapped out. I thought I knew what I wanted, and when things didn't work out, I realized that I had it all wrong. I realized I wanted something different altogether. I wanted something more…"

"And what is that?"

"I'm looking at it."

He leaned in and kissed her once softly, asking for permission with his expression. To his surprise, she kissed back. Hard. Relentlessly.

She climbed on top of him and pulled her tank top over her head. Jack leaned up, unfastened her bra, and took one of her breasts in his mouth and sucked hard. He pulled back, released her, and took the other in his mouth, giving it the same attention. Amelie ran her fingers through his hair, then grabbed a fistful of his hair and pulled it, forcing his face upward toward her. He grabbed her chin and sucked her bottom lip before releasing it and searching her eyes. "What about this guy you're seeing? Is it serious?"

She smiled and then trailed kisses down his neck. "Does it seem very serious to you?" she murmured, sucking on and then nipping his neck with her teeth. And just like that, Jack had had it with her smart mouth. All of a sudden, he had something to prove. He wrapped his arm around her back and lowered her to the bed. She perched herself up on her elbows as she watched him fumble with her shorts. With one hand, he unbuttoned them, and with the other, his own pants. He slowly pulled them down her legs, stood up, removed his, and then promptly buried his head between her thighs. Amelie moaned, dug her fingers into his scalp, and arched her back. Jack didn't stop until she begged him to fuck her. He obliged as she called out his name again and again and again. After they had finished in unison, they laid there, silent and sweaty, staring at one another until the light began to fade.

"Jack?"

His eyes widened, but he didn't speak.

She smiled a devious smile. *That smile he'd always loved.* "I'm really glad you came."

He leaned in and kissed the tip of her nose. "Me, too, kid. *Me too.*"

Acknowledgments

Most importantly, I'd like to express my gratitude to those who inspired me to write this story. You know who are. ☺

Thank you to Rogena Mitchell for the arduous job she did editing, and for pointing out with all of the grace in the world what was needed to polish my manuscript.

Once again, many thanks to Lisa Wilson of Pixel Pixie Design for being not only an amazing person but truly brilliant at all things design. More importantly, for not murdering me when I insisted we start over.

Thanks to the first readers: Monica, Denise, Dara, Heather, and Hunter. As ever, I appreciate your input and the motivation to keep going.

Last but certainly not least, I want to thank the readers. For every kind note, for every review, for simply reading… you guys are everything. Thank you.

Also by Britney King

Bedrock

Breaking Bedrock

About the Author

Writer. Wife. Mama. Expert juggler. Britney lives with her husband, five children, two dogs, and a cat in Austin, Texas. You can find her blogging on her website and she would love it if you'd connect with her on Facebook and Twitter.

www.BritneyKing.com

https://www.facebook.com/BritneyKingAuthor

www.Twitter.com/BritneyKing_

Made in the USA
San Bernardino, CA
16 November 2015